SONG OF NIGHT

CITY OF NIGHT
BOOK 2

AURORA GREY

BOOKS BY AURORA GREY

The City of Night Series

(A Crowns of Aureon Series)

City of Night

Song of Night

The Dark Fae Guardian Series

(A Crowns of Aureon Series)

House of Gilded Nightmares

Court of Bone and Amethyst

Lord of Broken Memories

The Raven Society Series

Hot Hex

Hex on the Beach

Hex in the Highlands

Viking Hex

Revenge Hex

www.auroragreyauthor.com

AUREON

VYRIN'S CASTLE

CYRENA

...RN FOREST

REBEL CAMP

CITY OF NIGHT

ILLIARE

N

I have dreamed a thousand times about what lies beyond the Waste. Ten thousand times, even. But never, in all those imaginings filled with desperate longing, did I envision it like this.

Asher standing a few feet away, his hatred of me forgotten in the moment.

Kieran's men, hands locked around my arms as they stare in shock.

The air, thick with dust and a shimmer of wild magic from the explosion. The explosion that blasted a rift through the never-ending gray mist surrounding the City of Night. Never-ending, that is, until *now*.

After more than two hundred years we know the answer to the question that has haunted us all: is there anyone alive on the other side of the Waste?

I wince as another blast of sound cuts through the

sparkling violet light, a sound that this time is unmistakable. Horns of battle, several blown in unison. The answer to our burning question, traveling now at great speed through the rift.

Whatever it is coming toward us is still two or three miles off, a dark blot in the distance, causing the mist to swirl skyward as it passes. How long had Asher and I been unconscious after the blast? It must have been longer than I thought, for someone—something—to be approaching the city so quickly.

Asher turns, his eyes catching mine for a moment, a fire of such intensity it makes my stomach flip. I want to go to him, to stand at his side, but in the next moment he wrenches his gaze from mine and locks it on his brother.

"We need all warriors to the rift immediately," he growls.

"You don't give orders around here anymore," Ellielle says, landing next to Kieran in a whoosh of blue-gray wings. "You are no longer Lord of Night."

Asher's face twists in anger. "Are you willing to forfeit the city because of your conceit?"

"Houses Animus, Angelus, and Syreni can face this threat without your help," Kieran says, arms crossed over his chest.

Ellielle's eyes are cold and deadly as she pins her gaze onto Asher. "Your forces are all but decimated anyway."

The emotion drops from Asher's face and my gut does another somersault. Is she bluffing?

Kieran and Ellielle bark orders to their warriors and

within minutes, the courtyard where Ellielle's weapon detonated is filled with not only crumbled stone and debris, but several hundred angels and shifters. The hum of their magic fills the air, reminding me that mine is gone. Mine and Asher's both, somehow stripped from us when the explosion occurred. It feels like a part of my soul is missing.

Without my connection to my magic, to Night, and with Asher's withdrawal at what he perceives as my betrayal, I feel a cold emptiness spreading through my body, like I'm filled with nothing but icy spiderwebs.

How did everything go so terribly wrong?

An eternity seems to pass as we wait. Slowly, the thing moving down the rift gains shape until I see what appears to be four galloping horses with riders carrying white flags. As they come closer, I can make out additional details: the strangely glowing bronze coats of the mounts, the red tunics of their riders, some sort of white emblem across their chests.

They head straight for us without slowing in the slightest as they pass into the city and cut through the path of collapsed buildings. When they get fifty feet from our position, they rein in their horses hard. The beasts are all foaming at the mouth, their chests covered in flecks of it. But these are no ordinary horses, they stand at least a foot taller at the withers. Their coats aren't the only thing with a metallic tint, their eyes are the same color, liked melted coins.

My hands itch for a weapon. Without my magic, I very

much desire a dagger. But I wait because the flags of the riders are white, and there's nothing a citizen of Night knows better than the diplomacy of war: as envoys, they are not to be harmed.

The four horses line up in a row facing us. Tension laces the air thicker than the dust still swirling across the courtyard. Behind me, the warriors shift their weight, swords and spears clinking in restless hands.

"Citizens of Illiare," calls one of the riders. His skin is very pale, and his hair golden. "We come to deliver a message from our king, Vyrin, ruler of the Flame Sea, the Thorn Forest, and all the lands of Cyrena."

A couple feet to my left, Asher stiffens, and I hear a low growl rise from Kieran's throat. They know of this king?

"The son of the demon lord will travel to our kingdom to parlay with King Vyrin. He may bring one advisor. Refusal of this visit will be considered an act of war."

The pale rider scans his gaze over the row of us: Ellielle, Kieran, Asher, and another dozen of their warriors. When his eyes reach mine, it feels like a shadow has blotted out the sun.

"You have until sundown tomorrow to comply."

I finally catch sight of the emblem the riders wear on their tunics, as well as emblazoned in black upon the white flags. It's a circle made of thorns, like a crown, with a single rose in the center. For some reason, looking at it makes me shiver. Or perhaps it's just the general hostility of the messengers, a hatred that radiates from them palpably.

"Consider your message received," Asher says, his voice dark and deadly.

The riders do not wait further. They spin their mounts and spur them back into a gallop. Within moments they're out of the city, their huge horses eating up the ground with incredible speed.

"Why did they call us citizens of Illiare?" I ask. "And who is this king—Vyrin?"

"You seem to know him, Kieran." Ellielle jerks her head toward my former mentor and commander. She must have heard the noise he made. "And you, Asher—I can only assume you are the son of the demon lord?"

My eyes flick between Asher and Kieran. I know they're brothers, but it's a secret from centuries ago that they keep well-guarded. The leaders of the other houses of Night do not know.

"I know of King Vyrin," Kieran responds. "His people fought ours before we were trapped within Night."

He's an excellent liar. I've experienced that firsthand—he'd kept so many things from me over the years.

Asher's words come out in a low rumble, as if he were the dragon shifter rather than Kieran. "Vyrin was the greatest enemy we ever faced. Back when this place was called Illiare."

He looks down, his gaze unfocused for a moment, clearly reliving past memories. When he looks up again, his jaw rolls in anger.

5

"It was Vyrin who started the war that set our people against each other in the first place, house against house, brother against brother. He is ancient... I do not know how old exactly, but he likes to claim that he was born when the world was born. His magic is vast beyond description." His eyes rake over the crowd, carefully avoiding both me and Kieran. "And yes, I am the son of the demon lord he refers to."

A grim hush falls over the courtyard as everyone contemplates what this means.

"We will adjourn to my tower to strategize," Ellielle says, gesturing to her warriors. Her gaze lands on me. "Except the shadow witch, of course. I trust you know what to do with her?" She looks disdainfully over at Kieran.

"I do indeed." He smirks, but he doesn't look at me. He looks at Asher when he says it. "Most people go mad within the first week in my prison cells in the old tunnels. Lack of light and all. But our Zara likes the dark."

"As long as I don't have to look at your lying face," I snarl.

Several of the Animus warriors—warriors I'd spent the last decade of my life fighting beside—grab me roughly and drag me away.

I don't struggle this time—I'm too numb to fight anymore. But I do look back, once, at the edge of the courtyard, to see if I can catch a final glimpse of Asher. He's facing away from me, but as if sensing my gaze, he turns and his eyes catch mine instantly.

They burn with such intense fury it feels like an arrow in the gut.

And then he spins and stalks away, surrounded by Ellielle's guards.

CHAPTER
TWO

ASHER

I find myself seated at a long table crafted of translucent grayish quartz, facing the angel who imprisoned and tried to kill me the day before, and my brother, who has attempted to murder me more times than I can count. Not to mention sending one of his spies to seduce me.

Or was that last part just Zara's sick addition to her mission?

Rage simmers in my veins, burning like fire. I relish the pain, because the pain and the anger keep me safe from the torment twisting around my heart like a wolf trap. Just hours before, I'd asked Zara to rule by my side. And now *this*.

The battle, the explosion, my ancient enemy rising from the ashes like a fire bird. None of it compares to Zara's betrayal.

It's all I can do not to lunge across the table and slit

Kieran's throat. This is worse than centuries of rivalry and failed assassinations. Sending Zara to spy on me, to gain my trust, to make me feel things I've never felt in my very long life…he couldn't have planned a more perfect pain if he had the rest of eternity to orchestrate it.

"So," Ellielle says, her fingers steepled on the rough-hewn table, wings folded behind her. "Tell me everything you know about King Vyrin. What kind of magic does he possess? How large is his army? What is Cyrena?"

I forget sometimes that Ellielle is barely past a century in age. All the beings in Night—Daemonium, Incantrix, Animus, Angelus, and Syreni—have the capacity to live for centuries upon centuries. But the war claims so many that few live that long anymore.

Kieran, of course, stays silent and lets me answer. Since we're pretending I'm the only son of the demon lord. The others at the table, a couple of Ellielle's advisors and one of Kieran's, haven't a clue, either.

"It's been over two centuries," I growl. "So, naturally, I don't know what has transpired beyond the Waste since that time."

Ellielle makes an impatient sound in her throat. I pin her in a burning gaze and continue.

"What I do know is that Vyrin attempted to claim my father's realm—Illiare, as it was called then. Both Illiare and Cyrena are realms within this continent. Aureon, it is called."

I receive several strange looks. We've been cut off from the rest of the world for so long that almost no one knows the names I'm using. All we have known for more than two centuries is Night.

"This all happened probably four hundred years ago," I say. "More than a century before I was born. The resulting war went on for so long that eventually it caused unrest within our own borders. The four houses that had once shared this land peacefully began to fight amongst themselves, bickering over war strategy and which house had lost the most warriors."

"But what *is* Vyrin?" Ellielle leans forward across the table, her frenetic energy palpable in the air, her eyes bright. "Is he like us? From one of the five races?"

My eyes meet Kieran's for the briefest of moments across the table. It's not missed by the angel, however.

"What?" Ellielle hisses. "You know something of this, too, Kieran?"

"Not as much as Asher, but I remember the tales as a child." Kieran pauses a moment, shifting in his chair. "Vyrin claims that his race is the original line... and that all of us descend from him."

Everyone around the table stiffens, varying shocked expressions on their faces.

"And what race, pray tell, is that?" Ellielle growls.

"The Fae," I say softly.

Silence falls for several long moments, and I can feel everyone's hearts beating, the blood racing in their veins. Because tales of fae have been passed down for centuries... every child hears them growing up. Tales of their magic and their cruelty and their wicked souls.

"But... it can't be true, can it?" Ellielle asks, looking around the table for someone to correct me.

I shrug. "I don't know, and honestly, I don't care. Truth or fiction, he used that claim as his reason for declaring war on Illiare, which he claimed to be rightfully his. And it's that war that led to this day: our four houses trapped for the last two centuries within the boundaries of the Waste, fighting amongst ourselves just as treacherously as Vyrin fought against us before." I smile, grim and without mirth. "Fae or not, it is clear our people share the same lust for bloodshed."

"So, his magic, then, Vyrin—"

"It is unlike any power I've ever witnessed." I blink a moment, lost in contemplation. We've been trapped within Night for so long that Vyrin had all but vanished from my memory. I'd forgotten, because *I* have been the most powerful thing in existence the last two centuries. Until Zara came along, of course. "I once witnessed him in battle...he has power more vast even than my own."

"You mean, the power you once had," Kieran says, his words blade-edged.

"Right you are." I nod and pin a burning gaze on Ellielle. "Thanks to you, for creating and then detonating the magical weapon I warned you not to use. We are now facing the greatest threat our people have ever encountered and I am without an ounce of magic because of your foolish pursuit of power."

Ellielle stands, her jaw tighter than a drawn crossbow.

"I think, my lord, that perhaps you need some blood. You seem rather on edge."

I stand, too, my gaze sweeping between her and Kieran. "I'm the one thing that could have saved us against this threat. The two of you plotted against me, and I hope you can see that you dug your own grave. Now you can go rot in it for all I care."

"Asher!" Ellielle snaps. "A word in private?"

She spins and leaves the room, stepping into a narrow passage covered partially by thick velvet curtains. I don't hide the growl that rumbles through my chest as I follow her. I shove through the curtain and see Ellielle standing a dozen paces down the hall in a shadowy alcove. Stalking toward her, I clench and unclench my fists. I'm so mad it's a good thing I don't have my magic right now, or this whole tower would be nothing but a pile of rubble.

"Why did you detonate the weapon?" I snarl.

"You're in no position to be demanding answers—or anything else from me," Ellielle snaps, her wings flaring out.

"On the contrary." I cross my arms over my chest. "I'm the only one our enemy will parlay with, so, magic or not, I'm the only one who can save this city. Now answer my question."

The angel glares at me a moment. "The weapon malfunctioned. It wasn't supposed to detonate at all."

"Not surprising. I warned you not to trap the wild magic like that." I pace back and forth across the hall, fury boiling in my blood. "If what you say is true about annihilating my warriors, I will let King Vyrin take this place and I will watch you all *burn*."

"The battle still rages on as we speak," Ellielle says. She pauses for a long moment. "Perhaps we can make some sort of arrangement."

I stop pacing. "What sort of arrangement?"

"The one you so rudely refuted the first time I asked." She pins me in a gaze sharp enough to cut diamonds.

My mouth falls open. "You still wish to be married? After everything that's happened?"

"I would rather cut out my heart with my own dagger than marry you, Asher," Ellielle says softly, eyes glowing. "But now, more than ever, Night needs unity. We cannot face this threat from Cyrena without it. Houses Angelus and Daemonium together, however, stand a chance."

I stare at her for several long moments. "You will call a halt to the battle and swear your loyalty to House Daemonium for the next three centuries."

"One century, and we have an accord."

She extends her hand, and after a moment I grab it, squeezing hard enough to break her bones had she not deflected me with magic.

"Shall we drink on it?" Ellielle says with a smile, not in the least bit perturbed.

She calls to someone, and after a moment a woman steps from a doorway a bit further down the hall, an Incantrix judging by the purple hue of her eyes and the magic spiraling off her. The Incantrix approaches, and when she reaches my side, she pulls her hair away from her neck and exposes it for me.

A wave of hunger rushes through me. Ellielle wasn't wrong about that part—I *am* on edge. The blast from the magic weapon took more out of me than just my magic. I feel like I haven't fed in a hundred years.

I hesitate only an instant before stepping up closer to the Incantrix and bending her head away from me. She winces as my teeth slide into the soft skin of her neck and her blood fills my mouth, hot and metallic. I expect a wave of relief, satiation, but all I can see in my head is Zara. All I can think of is how her blood tasted, her magic flowing within it. The most enchanting elixir I've ever had… the moans she elicited as I fed from her, the feel of our bodies intertwined as we shared of each other.

The blood now coursing down my throat tastes like ash.

I recoil a moment, and I see Ellielle's face flash with surprise. This has never happened to me before. While Zara's blood is special, I've never *not* enjoyed someone's blood before. Not in all my centuries.

But I need sustenance, whether I like the taste of it or not.

I continue sucking until I feel the Incantrix buckle beneath me. Stepping away from her, I make sure she can lean against the wall on her own before letting go of her. Then I turn to Ellielle.

"Was that… to your satisfaction?" she asks with a cocked eyebrow.

I ignore her question and the hunger that still burns inside me. I should feel more energized from that feed. While blood is only a temporary fix, souls being what I truly need, blood usually takes the edge off.

I feel barely better than before.

I don't voice this, however. Instead I say, "We need to ride out and call a halt to the battle. I want to be sure my people are safe before we continue our plan to deal with Vyrin."

Ellielle smiles and nods. "Yes. But don't forget—they're *our* people now, Asher."

THREE

ZARA

I lose track of time beneath the earth. I know it's only been a few hours since I was dragged down here to the cells and thrown roughly to the floor, but it seems an eternity.

With my magic, the darkness was never truly *dark*. I could see just as well as during the day, and the velvety shades of night were comforting, warm almost.

Now, however, I am truly blind for the first time in my life. The blackness that envelopes me is so complete, I can't even see my hand in front of my face. I'd panicked the first few minutes after they'd thrown me down here, but I'd forced myself to breathe, to remember that the dark isn't any different than it's always been.

I am the one who has changed.

My body is covered in bruises from the Animus guards dragging me down here, making sure to bang me up as much as they could on the way. Then several of them stayed behind to throw balls of magic at me, taunting me for losing the great power that made me teacher's pet to Kieran. The others had always been jealous of my control of the wild magic. I've been an outsider in my own home from the moment I arrived. Never has that been more clear than today.

For the first time, I understand why people pray to the dark goddess, why they burn effigies in her name. Because when it seems that all hope is lost, the only thing left to do is surrender.

Kieran betrayed me.

Asher now hates me.

I'd been reunited with my sister whom I thought to be dead, only to then be knocked unconscious by an explosion which has brought enemies to our doorstep.

And my magic is gone. All in the course of a few short hours.

If there was ever a time to pray to a deity, it's now. I wonder, with a strange sense of surrealness, if the reason I never have before is because I had Night. That ever-present connection to the source of wild magic, that violet glow like a living thing beneath the city, vast and powerful. I'd never needed to believe in a higher power because Night was that power.

But now it's gone from me, and I don't know what I'm going to do if I don't get that connection back.

Magic is the only constant in my life, ever present and faithful. My magic brought me to Asher, bonded us in a way I've never experienced with anyone. Only days before

I'd desired nothing more than to dive one of my daggers deep into his heart, but Night had linked us together, woven our fates as one.

If nothing else, I need to explain everything to him. Tell him how Kieran lied to me, built and fanned the fires of my hatred. He told me for years that Asher killed my sister. I'd only come to learn the truth the night before... not even the whole truth—that Jaylen is actually alive. Had Kieran known that, too? My life has been such a tangled web of lies.

But Asher's hatred of his brother runs so deep, I'm not sure he'll ever forgive me.

Another long stretch of time passes. Is it day still, or has night fallen? Has Asher set forth through the Waste to meet with the king on the other side? I wonder what lies beyond... what the land is like, the people, the magic. Do they even have magic?

I'm so lost in thought that I don't hear the footsteps until they're nearly upon me, just a moment before a ball of flame flares, illuminating a pair of golden eyes.

We stare at each other for several long moments.

"It pains me to see you like this, Zara," Kieran says finally.

"We both know that's not true," I say, my voice a low growl.

"But it *is* true." He steps closer to the bars of my cell. The flames from the magic he holds in his hand flicker erratically, as if there's a draft down here beneath the earth. His jaw is tight, his eyes glittering with cold malice.

It's like he's a completely different person from the man I'd looked up to for the last decade of my life. The man I once thought I loved. Is this his true self, or had my decision to choose Asher twisted him into this cruel creature? A shiver runs over me.

"We could have ruled the Animus together, Zara," Kieran continues. "I wanted you by my side. And now that I've partnered with Ellielle, our houses won't be at war constantly as we were under my brother's rule."

"If you truly felt that way about me, you wouldn't have lied to me from the moment we met." There's so much rage carried on my words that they nearly burn my tongue. "You chose poorly. Back then, and now. Because Ellielle has brought an even greater enemy down on our heads."

"I lied for your own good." Kieran's lips are set in a thin, angry line. "You lied because…well, I'm curious. Do you really have feelings for my brother, or did you just think to make yourself his queen? Gain more power?"

I'm so angry I can't speak for a moment. "We've known each other a long time, Kieran. Since when have I been power hungry?"

"Maybe neither of us know the other as well as we thought we did," he says softly, and it's the first genuine thing he's said to me since I confronted him the night before.

I'm silent for several moments. "I didn't mean for this to happen. You know how much I wanted revenge…but we share a connection, Asher and I. Through our magic."

"You share nothing now," Kieran says, his face

twisting again, the moment between us broken. "Your magic is gone, and even if it wasn't, he'll never forgive you. Trust me, I know that feeling well."

"Isn't it you who started the feud first? You who attempted to kill your own flesh and blood?" I snap.

"I'm sure that's the picture he painted," Kieran snarls. "But once out of Asher's good graces, you are forever banished. My brother hates me more than anything, and now he will hate you with the same fervor."

He spins abruptly and stalks away from me, taking his anger and his light with him. As darkness closes in around me again, I swallow down the wave of panic that threatens to consume me. Not because I'm going to be down here again, sightless and alone. But because I'm terrified that his words are true.

Just as he reaches the end of the long passage, his magic just a small glow in the distance, he pauses and turns. His voice carries back to me, echoing against the earthen walls.

"I hope it was worth it, Zara. A few days of pleasure for a lifetime alone."

And then he is gone.

CHAPTER
FOUR

ASHER

My heart is in my throat as I ride out with Ellielle to call a halt to the battle. I pray we're not too late. That my warriors haven't been wiped out as she claimed earlier.

I'd worried that Falling Star and the Factionless would rise against us, but that seems a distant memory now. How long will Ellielle's union with the other houses hold? I know my brother won't be loyal to this truce for very long, though it's possible the Syreni will keep up their end of the bargain. They've always had the closest alliance with the Angelus since their territories are adjacent.

No, Kieran will keep up the game to dig the knife he'd buried in my back even deeper. But as soon as he sees an opportunity, he'll turn on Ellielle. Especially given this ridiculous marriage to align Angelus and Daemonium. Had she told him that little part of her plan? *Our people…* her words feel like molten lead in my stomach.

When the river comes into sight, I rein in my gelding as my eyes rove over the scene before me. Ellielle has brought an entourage of warriors, and she gestures to the two closest to her, each of whom carries a silver horn. They raise the instruments to their lips and let out a series of blasts, amplified with magic. The sound reverberates across the battle, cutting across the clang of weapons, the screams of horse and rider, the blasts of magic hitting stone and metal.

Like a slow wave moving across a lake, a ripple spreads across the carnage. Heads turn, warriors pause mid-blow. All eyes turn to me and Ellielle, mounted on our horses in front of an ancient cathedral. Behind us, Ellielle's warriors raise white flags.

Ellielle stands in her stirrups and her wings flare out behind her.

"Warriors of Night!" she calls. Her voice, like the horn blast, is carried by magic. "Our great houses have called a truce! I am here, side by side with the Lord of Night, to announce a joining of our houses, to bring peace to this city at last."

Ellielle looks to me expectantly. I wish nothing more than to tell my warriors to fight to their last breath, to take out as many enemies as they can before they fall, to end House Daemonium in a blaze of blood and glory. For a moment, my lips refuse to cooperate, rebelling against issuing the words I know I must.

But I want my people to survive. And I can only hope

there are enough of us left to fight another day, a day I am better equipped to lead them.

Which is something that, without my magic, I cannot do.

"House Daemonium!" I call. "Lay down your weapons and join me in celebrating this union of houses! We have fought long and hard, and now we have earned peace, if for only a moment. Because we face a greater threat, a threat from across the Waste. Night is no longer cut off from the rest of Aureon—outsiders have breached our city."

A clamor of shock and surprise moves across the crowd. I wonder now if any here would be alive had Zara and I not been standing near the site of the explosion. The wild magic seemed to bounce off of us and cut north through the Waste, when it should have cast a wider circle of destruction.

But did we save the city only for it now to be taken by Vyrin's armies?

Shoving down my doubts, I call out again to the waiting warriors. "I travel at dawn to negotiate an agreement with these outsiders. Until I return, we call a cease-fire between the houses of Night. Rest and feast in honor of this victory!"

Across the battlefield, I see warriors from the different houses looking at each other in confusion, no doubt wondering if this is some sort of trick or trap. But they cease fighting as commanded. I let out a breath I hadn't realized I was holding, and some of the tension within my body releases. My eyes wander over the space between the cathedral and the bridge, trying to count the number of Daemonium still standing.

"I'll need to meet with my generals," I say quietly to Ellielle. "They won't buy this otherwise."

She looks as if she might argue with me, but after a moment, lips pressed in a thin line, she nods. "Do what you must, but be quick about it. And don't even think about crossing me, Asher."

"Why do you think I would I cross you? You only tried to kill me, ambushed my people, and detonated a deadly weapon." I let every bit of acid and heat I feel burning in my stomach leak into my words. But then I shake my head. "No, *some* of us have honor. We have a deal. I won't go back on it."

I turn from her, ignoring the quiet string of curses she throws at my back. I squeeze my heels to my horse and move across the plaza, summoning my warriors as I go. Finally, near the bridge, I catch sight of Malara, and shortly after, Helios.

"My lord, what has happened?" Malara asks when I ride up.

"Not here," I say. "We ride to the palace. Then we have much to discuss."

An hour later we've gathered back at the Palace of Night. It seems an eternity since I left this place, my childhood home. We'd been sure Ellielle would detonate the weapon there, so we'd evacuated further from the river.

Coming back to our home should feel like victory, but it tastes like ash and bone in my mouth. We'd far from won the battle. I'd made a deal with a devil to fight something even worse. I'd lost my magic and Zara both. And hunger is gnawing me from the inside out...

When I'd first tasted Zara, I thought she was sent by the goddess. Her blood quenched my never-ending hunger in a way nothing else ever had. Which must be the reason for what I'm feeling now, this desire that burns through me like a thousand endless infernos. A longing for something perfect that I can *never* have again. It would be so much better had I never given in to my lust for her in the first place.

The whole reason my hunger has been so intense these past two hundred years, why I needed souls in addition to blood, is because I was the conduit to Night. Always holding back an overwhelming stream of wild magic to keep it from annihilating the city, as it had when I'd first summoned and then lost control of it. Since I've lost my magic, I'm clearly no longer that conduit.

What will happen to the city now that I'm not anchoring the magic?

As I stand in the courtyard of the palace, a cold wind whipping down on me from above, I feel more defeated than I ever have. Worse even than that dark day over two hundred years ago when the wild magic ravaged the city.

I make my way to the Chamber of Souls where I meet with Helios, Malara, and Aya Olora, telling them all that

27

transpired in the last few hours since the battle began. When I am finished, Malara pins me in her purple gaze.

"Where is the Incantrix Zara?"

"In the dungeons beneath the Animus compound," I growl. "Where she belongs."

Malara blinks, and Helios stiffens ever so slightly in surprise. They do not ask further questions.

"So, tomorrow you travel through the Waste to meet the king who battled your father hundreds of years ago," Aya Olora says. "What if it's a trap—an act of revenge against the son of his enemy?"

"Likely it is." I cross my arms over my chest. "But what choice do I have? If I do not go, it means certain war."

"It will mean war either way," Helios intones flatly.

"I have no magic," I growl. "No way to defend this city. If I can buy us time, be useful in any way by either my life or my death, I will do it."

"It's true it could buy us time," Malara says. "Especially if we're going to have to figure out a strategy with the other houses."

"I don't trust Ellielle not to slaughter us the moment it's convenient for her," Aya says quietly.

"Nor do I, but for the time being, she needs us," I respond. "She won't do anything rash until she knows what lies on the other side of the Waste. How big Vyrin's army is, what magic and weapons they possess."

"And you intend to actually go through with this marriage when you return?" Helios asks, one brow raised.

"*If* I return." I cast my gaze over the three of them. "That is further than my hope will stretch at the moment."

"Who will lead in your stead should you not return?" Malara asks.

My gaze flicks around the table. "You and Helios should make all decisions jointly if I do not return. Keep each other's wisdom. You'll balance each other out."

"And who will you take across the Waste?" Aya asks. "You should bring an advisor, as you were granted."

I shake my head. "I do not wish to condemn anyone else to what is likely to be a grizzly fate."

Silence falls between us for several long moments.

"You know that any of the three of us would travel with you to the end," Malara says.

"I do. And for that loyalty, I am eternally grateful." I stand up from the table. "I must return to the Angelus now. Aya, you will oversee the warriors while I convene with the other heads of house regarding defense of the city. Make sure they behave at the feast tonight. Malara and Helios will join me at Ellielle's tower."

I turn for the door and have taken two steps when a wave of hunger washes over me, so intense that I stumble into the wall, my fingers crushing the stone beneath my fingers. I shouldn't need blood this badly after receiving some from Ellielle's servant. My hunger shouldn't be growing like this...

"My lord—are you ill?" Aya asks.

A growl rumbles through me. "I'm fine."

I push myself upright and make my way from the room.

My vision pulses red with the intensity of my craving. Surely this is some aftereffect of the explosion and stripping of my magic. As much as I crave Zara's blood, I can't be craving it *this* intensely.

Can I?

CHAPTER
FIVE
ZARA

I'm dozing in the corner of my cell when the earthquake begins. At first the faint rumble feels like part of my dream, a dream of battle and blood and wings and death. A repeat of the morning's events running through my head. Angels hunting me. My horse flipping beneath me, a spear buried in her heart. The explosion of the magical weapon just feet away from us.

It's the last part I mistake the earthquake for.

But as the rumbling intensifies, it shakes me from my sleep. Bits of stone and plaster fall on my head from above, and the bars of my cell rattle and creak. I have only a moment to wonder what's happening before wild magic pulses through the city.

Even though I don't feel it within me anymore, I know instantly that's what it is. A flash of heat and violet light, like ten thousand bolts of lightning striking all throughout Night. We've always had these fluxes of magic that would leave people dead in its wake each time. Everyone used to blame the Lord of Night, saying he let the wild magic loose on purpose to terrify the citizens, to keep everyone in check. But I'd come to know Asher's secret, that he is the anchor of Night, the only thing standing between Night and its citizens, holding back the incredible well of wild magic trapped here.

Was the only thing standing between Night and its citizens.

I'd wondered fleetingly, after the explosion, if the magic had been freed. If maybe that's why Asher and I lost our magic, since the two of us had the strongest connection to Night. It would solve one problem, even if it created many others—if the magic was no longer trapped, we wouldn't have deadly power surges anymore.

But as the earthquake intensifies, it becomes clear that I was wrong. The wild magic is still very much trapped, and now it has no anchor, nothing to control the chaos. It's the most powerful flare I've ever felt.

For a moment, I wonder if the magic will claim me, the magic I've had a strange connection to my whole life. A secret I've guarded so closely, how I can *feel* Night moving, breathing almost, as if she is a living thing. Asher is the only one who knows my secret, as I am the only one who knows his. I'd taken it for granted, not having to be afraid each day that wild magic could consume me. Now that I'm separated from Night, from my magic, will it end me as it's ended so many countless others?

The earthquake grows in intensity as does the electric

feeling in the air, the searing heat, the pressure, as if the magic is crushing me…

But then the surge passes, and I am still alive.

I can't see anything in this lightless place, but after my heart stops racing, I can sense that something is different in my cell, a change in the airflow, perhaps. I get up and take a step closer to the bars of my cell. Another step. I stretch forward with my fingers, feeling along the cold metal with the tips of them. I'm so concentrated on what's in front of my face that I trip over the rocks at my feet.

My breath leaves my lungs in a rush as I lurch forward. I catch myself on the bars, fingers grasping them desperately to keep from falling. The last thing I need is to injure myself down here. I have no idea when Kieran or any of the other Animus are going to check on me again. And I'm not sure they'd care even if they did find me wounded. I manage to keep myself from hitting the floor, and in the process, as my body weight hits the bars, they shift underneath me and more pebbles fall onto my head.

I straighten quickly, getting my feet beneath me. Heart racing, I grab the bars again and pull. They're definitely out of place, I can move them several inches. The rocks I'd tripped over must have come loose from around them.

In the dark, I try to get a better look at how much of the ceiling has fallen, but I can't see that far. No matter… I take in a deep breath and aim a kick at the loose bars. They shift another few inches, and more bits of ceiling fall around me. Hopefully I don't cause this whole place to crash down, but within the glimmer of possible escape, I can't bring myself to care.

I take a couple steps back and come at the bars again, another kick but with a running start. This time the bars move a few more inches forward. I land in a crouch, keeping myself from hitting the ground just barely. Then I stand, carefully feeling along the bars to see how much of a gap I'd made. There may be enough room, just by a breath, for me to squeeze out.

I step into the triangle-shaped space I'd made, pressing my body into the narrow V between the bars. One arm and one leg stretch through to the outside of the cell. Then I begin to shimmy my upper body through the gap. I suck in my breath, wincing as the metal pinches my chest, pressing into the bruises the guards gave me. For a moment, I don't think I'm going to fit. My heart pounds, my chest crushed so tightly between the metal that for a moment I can't even draw breath.

And then I am through.

I am free.

Sucking in a lungful of air, I move slowly down the passage toward the exit, mindful of the possibility of more fallen rocks. I'm located in the most subterranean level of the prison cells, with no other prisoners. But I know that as I travel toward the surface there will be others, and there will be guards. Without my magic, I'm nearly defenseless.

Nearly.

When I reach the end of the passage and climb the steps to the next level, I'm greeted with the flicker of torchlight. Not much, but enough. A quick glance down the row of cells before me shows that this level, too, is empty. I quicken my steps to the nearest torch and blow out the flame, then lift the metal holder from the wall. It is heavy and will make a fine club. I'd rather have my daggers, but those had been taken from me.

Weapon in hand, I jog down the passage until I reach the next set of steps. I slow to a walk and creep up and around the corner carefully. There are more torches lit on this cell block, and after a moment for my eyes to adjust, I see that the cells are mostly full. There's also a guard at the opposite end of the passage.

I'd lived for so long with the ability to bend shadows that I'd taken it for granted. Before, this would have been an easy task. Now, I have to make it down a corridor fifty paces in length without any of my cell mates calling for our captors.

Or just run like hell and use the element of surprise to my advantage.

Taking a deep breath and murmuring a prayer to the dark goddess, who clearly had a hand in my escape, I step around the corner and sprint for the guard at the end.

Cries ring out on either side of me, but the guard doesn't have much time to prepare before I leap for him, swinging my makeshift club in an arc that knocks him unconscious. I don't stop. I dash up the stairs as fast as I can, because there's one more level before I reach the surface, and the noise below has no doubt alerted the last of the guards.

I may not have my magic, but I have a storm of fury, betrayal, and anguish pent up inside of me. The next sixty seconds passes in a blur of fragmented images. The flicker of torches. The open mouths and rattling throats of the other prisoners as they scream. The surprised expressions of the three guards as I charge them. The glimmer of moonlight coming down the stone steps from the courtyard above.

And then there are three bodies lying at my feet.

Not dead, but bleeding and not moving anytime soon.

I cast them only a moment's glance. The last bit of nostalgia in my heart had been beaten out by the guards when they brought me here. My feet carry me the last few steps out into the open air above.

When I step out of the arched stone doorway, I come face-to-face with Kieran.

He doesn't wear the expression I'm expecting. It's not one of anger, but one of panic. "The earthquake," he says. "I thought you were…"

His words fall off, and then his jaw tightens as he sees the bloody piece of metal in my hands. But even if just for that fleeting moment, in his eyes I'd seen the answer to one of the questions that's been haunting me.

"I don't want to hurt you, Kieran," I say softly. "I didn't then, and I don't now."

"*You* hurt *me*?" He laughs, and his inner dragon surges to the surface, his golden eyes glowing in the darkness.

The part of him that cares for me is gone again. I don't hesitate—I swing the torch and hurl it at his face. It rotates twice in the air before colliding with his cheekbone. Kieran flies backward, and I am running before he even hits the ground. I know that I'm not going to make it far. But I'm not going to stand here and let him have me. Maybe, if he's angry enough, he'll kill me and get it over with. All I know is that I'm not going back beneath the earth for the rest of my days.

It's not the dragon behind me, however, that I have to worry about.

I hear the beating of wings just a moment before a shadow falls across me from above, and then I'm lifted from the ground and carried off into the sky.

CHAPTER
SIX
ASHER

t's all I can do not to drain the blood from everyone at the table. Their souls would be better, but without my magic I can't summon them.

Ellielle sits directly across from me at the other end of the long table. Her advisors sit on each side of her. Lord Octavius of the Syreni is there as well, with his own advisors. Malara and Helios sit at my right.

We've been gathered here in Ellielle's tower for over an hour. We were on our way to the meeting when wild magic ripped through Night. An angel just feet away from me was eviscerated on the spot. We'd passed buildings toppled by the quake and places where the earth had been cracked open like a ripe melon, strange mist rising from below. Upon reaching the tower, I'd been told Kieran was missing. Ellielle sent several warriors to try to find him, and since then we've been waiting.

All the while, my hunger grows, seemingly by the minute.

"We'll just have to get started without him," Ellielle finally says, narrowing her eyes and glancing over her shoulder out into the hall one last time. "If he survived the surge, the Lord of the Animus will have to join us later."

It would be the utmost of irony if after all these years battling with my brother, it was the wild magic that finally claimed him. And of course, I wonder about Zara, in a cell beneath the earth during an earthquake. Not that her fate means anything to me. But just the thought of her makes my hunger increase.

I'm gripping the edge of the table so tightly that the white of my bones shows through my skin. A small rumble moves through me.

Ellielle levels her gaze to mine. "Asher, are you alright?"

"Never better," I growl.

Next to me, Malara's attempt to not make eye contact is painfully obvious.

"Okay then, let's begin…"

We make it through a half hour of battle strategy before footsteps are heard coming down the hall. I look past Ellielle, expecting to see Kieran approaching at last, but it's not my brother. It's an angel.

An angel carrying a very angry Incantrix.

The angel's wings flare out as he enters the room and deposits Zara on the stone floor with a bone-crunching thud. As she climbs slowly to her feet, her tunic slides down and I can see she's got a purple bruise across one shoulder. Was that from the earthquake or did someone hurt her? I forget for a moment that she betrayed me as rage burns through my blood. But another sensation races right alongside that emotion…

Hunger.

A growl escapes me and I stand abruptly, shoving my chair back as I push off from the table. It's a combination of fury at the idea of her being mistreated, and also the deepest, darkest of cravings. I realize all eyes are pinned to me rather than Zara.

"What is she doing here?" I snarl, trying to cover my reaction with something more appropriate.

"I caught her escaping the Animus prison," the angelic warrior says, crossing his arms over his chest.

Zara glowers at the winged creature, her fingers twitching at her sides as if wishing they held a weapon.

Ellielle makes a sound of disappointment, something between a groan and a *tsk*. "It seems the Lord of the Animus has a problem containing completely unmagicked and defenseless prisoners."

"Ask the guards how defenseless I was," Zara says in a low, deadly voice.

"And about Lord Kieran…" the angelic warrior begins.

I slam my hands down on the table. "But my question remains—why is she *here*?"

Malara and Helios both stare at me, barely contained shock on their faces. I'm losing this battle of wills with myself, the hunger all-consuming, blinding…

"I asked Yadriel to bring her here when the others went to look for Kieran," Ellielle says. She locks eyes with me. "I think we may have a use for our little Incantrix. Perhaps we can discuss it privately?"

Ellielle stands and walks from the room. I suppress another growl. She's enjoying these little humiliations in front of the other heads of house, that much is clear.

"Bring the girl," she calls over her shoulder, to me or to Yadriel, I'm not sure.

Zara saves us the trouble of figuring it out, striding after Ellielle without a glance at either of us. I follow the two women down the corridor outside the meeting hall. Ellielle steps off into a side room which appears to be a small library. When I enter, she closes the door behind us and I stalk past her and Zara and begin pacing on the far side of the room, as far away from them both as I can be.

"Explain this," I snap.

"Call it a woman's intuition," Ellielle begins, a smirk on her face as she sweeps her gaze between me and Zara. "But you didn't seem satisfied with the blood I provided you earlier. And being as how you have no magic to claim souls, I thought I would test a theory."

"What theory?"

A few feet away, Zara stiffens, and Ellielle's cruel smile widens. She doesn't answer me verbally but simply turns to Zara, closes the three-stride distance between them, and in one swift movement, draws a tiny knife and slices it across Zara's neck.

The scent of Zara's blood turns the whole room to crimson.

I blur across the room, an animalistic roar ripping out of me. I stop myself at the last second, my hand an inch from encircling Zara's throat. My entire body is shaking violently with the urge to drink from her, to taste her, to *claim* her.

"Hmm." Ellielle makes a gesture with one hand, a casual flick of the fingers. "Seems I was right."

"You do not know what you're doing, angel," I snarl.

Zara is staring at me, eyes wide, not moving a muscle. She knows if she tries to run now, she is dead.

"I know *exactly* what I'm doing," Ellielle says. "I'm saving this city. Something you can't do if you lose control. You think you can cross the Waste and negotiate with our greatest enemy in the state you're in?"

"You've overstepped, Ellielle." I turn to face her, my inner demon blazing behind my eyes. Magic or no, I am still darkness and flame, and I can see in her expression that she knows it.

She swallows but her posture never weakens. "Feed on her. Now."

I turn back to Zara, my control hovering on the thinnest razor's edge. Even with everything that's happened, using her as a blood bag doesn't feel right. Before, when I'd fed on her, it hadn't been about basic need. It had been an entirely different kind of craving.

Zara meets my gaze steadily, and with one hand, she pulls her hair to the side so I can access her neck. "She's right," she says softly. "You're crossing the Waste tomorrow. You need to be sharp."

My willpower shatters and I yank Zara against me, one hand encircling her waist, the other sliding into her dark hair. I groan as my lips meet the soft skin of her neck, her blood racing hot and fast beneath it. My teeth extend, puncturing her flesh, and ecstasy rolls through my body as her essence pours into my mouth. My magic may be gone, but Zara *is* magic. Pure magic.

A small moan escapes Zara as I drink from her, her body shuddering against mine. I can feel the curve of her breasts, her hips, her thighs pressing into me. Energy floods through me and the agonizing hunger falls away. I hate that she makes me feel this way, because she can never be mine. Not anymore. Not after being *his*.

My body, however, has no such compunction. I can feel myself hardening like a sword, pressing into Zara's belly. She shivers against me again, and my fingers dig more tightly into her. I suck at her neck and she moans, louder this time. I want to taste her everywhere, penetrate her in every possible way...

The thought shakes lose the hold of my hunger. I gain control of my senses and step away from her. This cannot be. Nothing like that can exist between us ever again.

Zara averts her eyes from mine and takes another step away from me, her hand moving to her bleeding neck. Ellielle steps forward and hands her a square of cloth.

"Well, that was...enlightening," the lady of House

Angelus says softly. "I can see now why Zara made it into your inner circle so very quickly."

I scowl over at her, wiping blood from my mouth with the back of my hand. "Enough with your commentary, Ellielle. My hunger is abated now. You can send Zara back to Kieran and we'll continue our plans for dealing with Vyrin."

Ellielle laughs. "Oh, I think not, Asher. We can't risk you going into Cyrena and having another issue with your hunger." Her eyes dart to Zara. "It seems your little witch is the only thing that will satisfy you these days."

"Meaning what?" I take a threatening step toward Ellielle. "I'm not taking Zara with me."

Ellielle just steps toward me herself, so close that her chest nearly bumps mine. "That's precisely what you're going to do."

"Think again," I snarl.

"I'm not asking, Asher. We're engaged now, remember? Consider it a condition of our arrangement."

Beside me, Zara goes still as a statue.

"You can't add conditions after we've already made our agreement," I snap.

"Be reasonable. You know I'm right." Ellielle sighs and strides for the door. "I'm not going to waste further time arguing the point. You need the witch. At dawn, you will begin the journey across the Waste together."

When she reaches the doorway, she turns and shrugs. "And, if you're going to lose control and kill someone, it might as well be someone we don't care about."

SEVEN

ZARA

I'm not sure what's worse... Asher's icy silence or the misty stretch of toxic wasteland as far as the eye can see.

Fog roils like a nest of serpents in all directions save for the narrow path, no more than twenty feet wide, made by the explosion of wild magic. I don't know why the mist hasn't moved back in to fill the void... it's walled up on either side of the gap, almost perfectly vertical as if held in place by invisible hands.

It's unnerving to say the least.

And I'm about to travel into the heart of it.

Asher and I are mounted, him on his gray gelding, me on a black mare. Behind us, an entourage of warriors is there to bid us farewell. Ellielle, Malara, Helios, and several dozen others, everyone coming here at first dawn to see us off. There's a morbid quality to it, an air of despair. No one thinks we're actually going to make it back alive.

I know from snatches of conversation I'd caught this morning that they spent most of the night finishing plans for the defense of Night against Vyrin's armies. Battle strategies and weapons inventory and contingency plans. We are a people well accustomed to war. The thing that's different this time is we're not battling each other.

I had not attended those meetings, of course, but spent the night locked in a tiny room at the top of the tower. Asher hadn't said a word to me after he'd fed. He'd simply walked from the room without a backward glance and left his betrothed to deal with me. Kieran hadn't shown his face either, though at one point I'd heard him and Ellielle arguing outside my room about the fact that she'd stolen me away from him. She of course pointed out that I'd already escaped when her angel collected me.

Which probably explains why he's conspicuously absent from the farewell gathering.

"I wish you swift travels," Ellielle calls from where she stands a few feet away, black hair blowing in the breeze. "The fate of our city lies in your hands. May the dark goddess be with you."

Murmurs of farewell shift over the crowd. I turn my gaze forward again, down the eerie path ahead, and urge my horse into the Waste, Asher at my heels. I cast no final glance at the city I grew up in, the city I love. And I cast no final glance at the people standing there, because I have no one.

We ride in silence for two hours, until Night can no longer be seen behind us.

It's strangely quiet, which only increases the sense of foreboding that creeps into my bones. I glance up occasionally at the walls of shifting fog on either side of us, which rise a couple hundred feet into the air. The ground beneath my horse's hooves is gray and dry and cracked. There is no evidence of anything that was once here: not a tree stump, not a dwelling, not a hill or a riverbed.

But I suppose nothing is better than something, when those somethings are rumored to be ravenous monsters. I'd grown up hearing tales of them, but it seems maybe we've gotten lucky. Or maybe the monsters can't come near the rift created by the explosion, repelled from it somehow as the mist is. Repelled by the lingering magic that hangs in the air.

It doesn't even smell like anything here, not even earth.

Every time I cast my eyes over to Asher he is staring steadfastly ahead, jaw tight, eyes full of anger. Even his posture is rigid in the saddle, his hands gripping the reins too tightly. If I had ventured a hope that maybe the night before had changed anything, I was clearly foolish. His body may have reacted to me, but his mind and his heart clearly do not align.

I make it another hour before my resolve breaks.

"You didn't even give me a chance to explain myself," I say, my voice low and controlled, but loud enough to carry the three feet that separates our horses.

49

Asher doesn't respond and doesn't look at me, but I know he heard by the way his jaw rolls.

"I was assigned to spy on you. That is true," I continue. "But then things changed."

The silence between us is deafening, as if a great wind were slicing down into the rift.

"Kieran told me you killed my sister when I was first captured by the Animus, after the prison camp. I wanted revenge on you for the last decade, ever since that moment. And then you killed Lyri. I was very justified in my feelings." I swallow and keep going. "But when I found out Kieran was your brother, I knew he'd been keeping things from me. And that's when everything began to unravel."

Asher's gaze cuts to mine with such force it feels like a physical blow. "Do you or did you ever have feelings for my brother? Do you love him?"

I know the truth is going to anger him, but I won't back away from it. I want him to know everything. Swallowing, I meet his eyes. "Once I… I thought I did. But—"

"That's all I need to know, Zara," Asher growls. "Nothing else matters to me." He pivots his gaze forward again.

"That was before I met *you*," I snap, anger rushing through me at his dismissal. "I realized then that my feelings for Kieran were nothing but a schoolgirl's admiration. I realized how depthless they were, compared to—"

"Compared to what?" Asher doesn't turn his eyes back to me. "I offered you a spot by my side, to rule Night with me, and you did not accept. Do not try to win me over now because everything was stripped away from you."

"That's not why," I growl.

But Asher spurs his horse into a gallop and leaves me behind in a swirl of dust.

EIGHT

ASHER

I f Zara knew how close I am to losing control, completely and irrevocably, she wouldn't risk following me. She'd turn around and head back to Night, or take her chances escaping through the Waste.

Either option is safer than I am.

It's not just that I'm still angry with her. It's this hunger inside of me, howling like a wolf. It'd come back the second I saw her this morning. The times I drank from her before it seemed to sustain me longer, but now it seems to have the opposite effect. It seems being in her presence only *increases* my hunger.

Ellielle knows she sent Zara to her death. Was it merely to get rid of the competition?

Not that Ellielle is any competition for my feelings for Zara—the feelings I used to have for Zara.

I gallop my horse until his breathing is labored and he's flecked with sweat and foam from his mouth. It's not far enough, but I'm not going to kill my horse. This whole mission relies on us reaching Vyrin's castle by sundown, and my horse isn't some sort of magical creature that can cover the distance their horses can in such a small amount of time.

When I bring my gelding to a walk, it's not long before I hear hoofbeats announcing Zara's horse coming up behind me. Anger flashes in my belly. She'd admitted she once loved Kieran. Any small hope of gaining my forgiveness had been shattered with those words. I can't believe I once trusted her so blindly. It was Night that made me so foolish, the connection we shared through our magic.

Maybe it's for the best that magic is now gone.

I'd rather live my whole life without an ounce of power than feel connected like that to Zara again.

But when she pulls her horse up beside me, the beast inside surges toward her, having no such hatred. I *want* her, more than anything in this cursed world, and I hate myself for it. A growl rises through my core and I stare steadfastly ahead, hoping for some sign that we're reaching the end of this journey. All I see, however, is the rift. Miles and miles and miles of it, straight as an arrow through the roiling fog.

"It's ironic you're so angry about my past feelings for Kieran when you struck up with Ellielle hours after asking me to rule by your side," Zara says by way of greeting.

White-hot rage simmers through my veins. "It is not wise to speak to me right now, Zara."

"The way I see it, I have nothing to lose," she snaps,

pinning her purple gaze on mine. "You clearly hate me for something that isn't my fault and can never be changed."

"You are extremely mistaken about what you could and could not lose." My hands grip the reins so tightly the leather cracks beneath my fingers and my horse prances, sensing the dark fury within me.

"I don't have to pretend to work for you anymore. Or obey you." She lifts her chin, the tendons in her neck tight, the column of her neck so pretty it makes my chest throb.

"You are in *danger* right now. Do you understand that?" My voice is shadow and flame, my inner demon so close to the surface my vision is turning red again. I may not have magic, but I'm still a predator. A predator with deadly instincts and abilities.

"I'm tired of your threats, Asher," Zara snarls. "If you drain me here in the Waste, you're not going to make it to Vyrin to negotiate a treaty. Ellielle was right about one thing—you need me."

My eyes cut to hers. "You mistakenly assume that I have *any* control over my hunger right now."

Zara's eyes flicker, doubt entering them for the first time.

"If you had any sense, you would leave now. Go far, far away from me and remain so for the rest of your life." And I mean it. I want her to leave. I may hate her, but I don't want her to suffer the fate that awaits us ahead. If she survives the next five minutes.

"I do have sense," she growls, "Which is why I'm

going to make sure we make it across the Waste so our people have some small chance of survival."

"We aren't going to negotiate anything with Vyrin. He's cruel and sadistic, and this whole thing is one big game to him." I look over and lock eyes with her. "You wanted me dead for so long. Now you're going to get your wish."

"Asher," she says, her eyes turning stormy and her lips trembling. "I—"

But I don't get a chance to hear what she has to say, because at that moment something leaps from the bank of fog to my left and knocks me off my horse.

It is a creature from the darkest of nightmares, a thing of coils and tentacles and fangs. Serpent-like and twice the size of my gelding, gray like the mist around us, except for its eyes. Its eyes glow an orange-blue like the heart of a flame, shifting and flickering like one, too. No legs or arms, just one long body with writhing, barbed appendages sprouting the length of it.

Before I even hit the ground it has those tentacles around me, crushing my chest like a vice. It lifts me, coiling its body, and moves me toward its open maw. A wave of putrid breath burns my eyes, and its teeth shine as if covered in venom. I struggle as my death stares me in the face from inches away.

And then the thing jerks back, letting out a hiss. Zara spins, withdrawing a dagger, and darts in again. She's nearly as fast as the monster, moving with a lithe grace, her face expressionless, devoid of fear.

The creature's grip loosens and I pull the sword at my belt, one of the weapons I'd brought since I have no magic. It's been a long time since I've had to use such a thing. Adrenaline rushing through my veins, I swing the blade down across the monster's middle, slicing it in half.

It screams and flails, but it doesn't die.

Where I'd chopped it, more tentacles spring out and it grows in length again, the end with the head lunging for Zara. The other piece of the thing disintegrates in a cloud of red-tinged toxic gas. I'm too close to get away in time and the stuff wafts over me, burning my skin and eyes. I let out a yell and stagger backward, partially blinded.

The battle comes in choppy flashes as I blink to regain my sight.

Zara and the serpent spinning around each other in a deadly dance.

The flash of her blade.

The glow of the beast's eyes.

Writhing tentacles encircling Zara's legs.

I force myself forward again, zig-zagging as my vision goes in and out. Zara's on the ground now. I see the thing dart its head down, but she dodges its ten-inch teeth. Her blade goes into the side of its neck, but it barely reacts.

It dives for her again, but this time my sword takes its head clean off. And when the head hits the ground, already growing more tentacles, I impale it through the top of the skull, clean through its brain. The monster finally goes still, its eyes staring sightlessly at Zara.

I lunge for her as it starts to disintegrate, rolling on top of her and away from the thing. We roll several feet across the sand, barely managing to avoid the poisonous gas left by the creature's carcass. When we finally stop moving, I'm lying on top of Zara.

We're both breathing heavily from the fight, and Zara's face is covered in dirt. I'm sure mine is even worse, my skin still burning from getting caught in the noxious gas. My vision is still blurry, but my other senses absorb everything. The racing of Zara's heart, the feel of her breath on my face. The curve of her hips beneath mine.

"Asher, your arm," she whispers.

I look down, realizing that in addition to being burned, I have a bloody gash down my bicep where I must have been impaled by the barbed tentacles. Pain lashes through my body as my adrenaline slows. It's more than the cut—there's clearly poison running through my veins.

And in that moment, as agony takes hold of my body, I lose the fragile control I've been holding on the hunger inside.

CHAPTER
NINE
ZARA

I watch Asher's eyes as he winces in pain and a tremor moves through his body. But then his expression changes, something wild and craven roiling beneath the surface. I have only an instant to realize what's happening before he sinks his teeth into my neck.

He is not gentle.

A cry escapes my lips, both pain and pleasure. Because even through my fear, even though I can tell he's lost control of his inner demon, even though my life is in grave peril, the bliss still sings through all of it.

Asher sucks hungrily at my skin, one hand twisted in my hair, holding my head in place, the other wrapped underneath my body, under the arch of my back, pressing me up into him. His cock lengthens against me and I shudder, hooking one leg up around his hips to press him harder into me.

He growls and sucks even harder for a moment. My

eyelids flutter, both from the wave of ecstasy, and because he's taken so much blood already in just a few moments. At the back of my mind, I know I should be scared. But I also know if I struggle right now, it's just going to trigger his animal instincts even more.

I move one hand to the back of his head, pressing his mouth even harder against me, and my other hand slides between our bodies to the waistband of his pants. My fingers move over the hard length of him and he shivers against me. A moan escapes his throat.

Asher's lips slide down my neck and he pulls my tunic aside, plunging his teeth into the soft, rounded top of my breast. I gasp as a fresh spike of pleasure moves through me, and Asher undulates his hips, grinding into me. Even fully clothed, I can feel the beginnings of that blissful little death rippling through my body.

I wrap my other leg around him and pull him even closer. "*Asher…*" I gasp.

He pulls back and his mouth finds mine, his tongue probing me with as much ferocity as his teeth had. I can taste my blood on his lips. His breath mingles with mine, and although no magic sparks between us, there's enough fire even so to burn the whole world down around us.

Another moan moves through me.

And then, abruptly, he pulls back.

He straightens, still straddling my hips. His brow furrows and the muscles in his jaw roll. He looks down at his arm, seeing that his wound has closed, my blood healing him. Even without magic, he apparently still has the healing abilities of a vampire.

"We need to keep moving," he says gruffly, standing and turning from me to go find his horse.

My heart is still racing, my breathing ragged. Slowly, I roll onto my knees and then climb to my feet. I stare at his back as he strides to his horse, who had the good sense not to run off into the fog. Mine is next to it, their eyes still wide with fear from the attack.

"So, you're just going to kiss me and then act like nothing happened?" I snarl.

Asher doesn't turn around, but his voice carries over his shoulder. "I fed, which is the whole reason you came along. This changes nothing between us."

"That was not just feeding, and you know it!" I stalk toward him, snatching the reins of my horse off the ground where they dangle.

"Oh, and you're now an expert on blood-drinking demons?" His brown eyes are cold as he meets my gaze.

"I know what I felt," I say softly.

"Feeding is a…full body experience." His tone is as frosty as his eyes. "It doesn't mean there are feelings involved. It's purely physical."

"I see." I turn away from him and mount my horse in one swift movement.

"You're lucky to still be alive," Asher growls.

"Oh, so now I'm supposed to thank you for not killing me?" I can feel blood dripping from the two puncture wounds on my neck, and I reach up to touch it without conscious thought.

Asher's face goes still. He pulls a small dagger from his boot, then cuts a piece of cloth from his tunic before handing it to me. "Here. Tie this around your neck."

I snatch the cloth from his hands and start tying it around my neck. He urges his horse forward and leaves me as I sit there trying to get it fastened securely. Fury flashes through me as I watch him go. And with that surge of raw emotion, I feel a flicker through my core. A flicker that feels like...

I focus on the feeling, but it's not my magic, not the flare of Night. Disappoint flashes through me, which on top of Asher's rejection sends a shiver of sorrow through my chest.

I'd do just about anything to get my power back, but clearly my longing is making my imagination run wild. I'm just as unmagicked as I was before.

The light in this place is so dim it's hard to tell what time of day it is, and I'm beginning to fear we're not going to reach the other side of the Waste in time. We've been riding for hours since the monster attack, alternating between cantering and walking the horses.

Of course, all that awaits me there is my death. Likely after an extended period of torture.

One of my earliest memories, over three centuries ago, is of Lord Vyrin. I'd been barely more than twenty. My father sent several emissaries to Vyrin's court to negotiate an agreement between our realms after Vyrin started encroaching on the boundaries of Illiare. I remember what came next with the same vividness as if it happened yesterday.

We sat in my father's throne room in the Palace of Night, though it was not called the Palace of Night back then. Then it was called the Royal Court of Illiare. My father and mother sat in the center of the dais, Kieran and I flanking them on smaller thrones. Four messengers in the blue livery of our house entered the long, marble-tiled room, carrying an ornate metal chest between them.

My father's eyes gleamed as they set the chest down before him. Based on his expression, I leaned forward in my chair, too, expecting a treasure of some sorts as an apology and a peace offering. Gold perhaps, or rubies or amethysts. With a nod, my father gestured for the messengers to lift the lid of the box.

For a moment, just the barest of moments, I thought it was rubies after all.

But then the scent hit my nose, the sharp tang of blood. My brain pieced together what I was seeing: severed body parts stuffed inside the chest, flesh and bone in sharp contrast with the crimson covering everything.

The emissaries we'd sent to negotiate peace.

That day I realized two things. First, that Vyrin was a sadistic sociopath who couldn't be reasoned with. And second, that sometimes violence is the only choice. Be powerful or be prey.

War had become my life from that moment forward. It drove my every move, fueled my obsession with deeper and darker magic, until a century later I unlocked the flood of wild magic that changed everything. Killed my father, turned my brother against me. Everything prior to that fateful day seemed a past life, something I'd locked away.

But now my past has come back to taunt me.

My enemy clearly has no time limit on his grudge, which is why I know this whole expedition is nothing but a sick and twisted game. I can't help but flick my gaze over to Zara, who is riding sullenly beside me. Killing her earlier would have been a mercy compared to what awaits us ahead. No matter how furious I am with her, I won't let Vyrin have her. Not someone like him.

I glance down at my arm, which is completely healed. In fact, my entire body is buzzing with energy after drinking Zara's blood. I'm grateful I still possess the natural healing abilities of a vampire because I'm quite certain I'd be dead otherwise. Though, I'm not sure Zara is going to let me feed on her ever again after what I said earlier.

It hadn't been a lie, not entirely.

With vampires, sexual arousal on behalf of the drinker is not uncommon. I've always been an exception, however, rarely feeling anything but guilt for my hunger. Zara's reaction to being consumed is also completely unique... her obvious pleasure makes it impossible not to want her in every way.

I'd almost lost control in two ways today. Both in draining her dry, and in ripping off every piece of clothing and entering her in the way that we both so desperately crave.

It makes me furious that I still want her in that way, knowing she'd likely given her body to my brother also. Made those same moans of pleasure...

"The horses have rested long enough," I say, and I kick my gelding forward into a canter.

We move at a faster pace for more than a quarter hour. The light ahead, far down the rift, begins to change. At first, I'm not sure if it's a mere trick of the eyes, delirium from riding for hours and hours. But as I keep straining my eyes, I see that it's definitely getting lighter in the distance. A golden light, as if…

As if the sun is setting beyond the Waste.

Zara sees it, too, and she moves her horse from its steady canter into an outright gallop.

I urge my gelding to follow, pushing him faster and faster until he's at his limit. It can't be more than five miles ahead. A sense of dread fills me as I lay low over his neck, his mane flying in my face, his muscles surging beneath me. If we miss the deadline by such a short window of time…

Perhaps it will anger Vyrin and he'll kill us quicker. Better than the alternative.

The ground is eaten up by my horse's hooves and within a few short minutes, we're approaching the end of the passage through the mist and fog. There isn't further time to speculate on what horrible things await us in Cyrena. Whatever happens now, it is upon us.

We surge through the opening on the other side of the Waste, and I see the outside world for the first time in over two centuries.

I rein in my horse and Zara does the same. As I gaze out across the scene before us, I hear a small exhalation of wonder escape her lips. She's never seen anything beyond Night, anything past the Waste that has entrapped us. Sometimes, I forget how very *new* she is.

My eyes follow hers from horizon to horizon.

Directly in front of us lie gently rolling hills of verdant green which stretch a half mile or so to sheer granite cliffs. Beyond the cliffs lies the ocean, an expanse of gray-blue waves which even from here can be heard crashing angrily against the shoreline. Far off, I see what might be a fishing boat bobbing on the water.

To the left a ways off is a forest which rises from the hills abruptly, black and twisted. There is nothing green about it, no leaves, no curling vines. It is made entirely of dark brambles covered in huge thorns that stick out like dragon's teeth, piercing the sky. There's a malevolence about it, as if it's trying to overcome the barriers which constrain it.

In the distance, a massive castle sits at the apex of the swelling hills, hanging over the sea cliffs. It actually looks more as if it's growing out of them, the stone trying to escape, just like everything else in this place. There is nothing symmetrical about the structure, no clean lines like my own palace. The walkways and parapets jut out at haphazard angles. White flags fly from its towers, bearing the house sigil of a rose encircled by thorns.

Above it all, the sun sinks low, nearly touching the far-off waves, painting everything in rose and gold. It's beautiful, and yet tinged with deep foreboding. Or perhaps I have been trapped in Night for so long that the outside world has taken on a sinister tone. I have lived too long behind impenetrable walls.

I look over into Zara's wide eyes. The sudden sense to protect her washes over me. Nothing good will happen here. I'd known it before, but now, seeing Vyrin's realm spread before me, I have absolute certainty that this place will be my grave.

"Zara," I growl. "I want you to turn around and ride back through the rift."

Her head whips to mine, and her eyes widen even more.

"You've gotten me this far. You did your job. But what lies ahead is not for you."

"What?" Her lips stretch thin, her eyes narrowing. "I'm not leaving."

I hear the blast of a horn from the castle, and in the distance, the gates open and several horsemen come galloping out. With their huge, magical beasts, they'll be on us in less than a minute.

"Vyrin is heartless and cruel. There will be no negotiations." I stab my finger back the way we came. "Go, Zara. Now!"

"Ellielle will kill me if I return without you," she snarls.

"Anything that angel can dream up will be a hundred times better than what this sadistic fae will do to us. I'm not asking, Zara. I *command* you to go."

I rein my gelding into her horse from the side, herding

her toward the rift. The cloud of dust in the distance is coming closer, and now I can hear hoofbeats.

"I don't work for you anymore, remember?" Zara's turns her mare and spurs her away from mine, breaking free.

"Goddess help me, Zara, if you don't go, I will *make* you go—"

But my words are cut short as Vyrin's riders burst into view over the nearest hill.

They gallop toward us, weapons drawn, and I realize I've just made the biggest mistake of my life.

CHAPTER
ELEVEN
ZARA

The riders on the strange bronze horses encircle us. Asher's gaze burns into mine, and I can tell he's furious I've defied him.

I'm not actually sure myself why I stayed.

Asher has made it clear that nothing I do can repair the damage between us. He's angry about something I have no control over, the fact that I spent half my life in House Animus and worked for his brother. That I'd once had feelings for Kieran before I even met Asher.

I'd had my chance to explain myself, and he'd rejected that explanation. *And* me. Just a handful of days ago, I hated this man with every fiber of my being. So why does it hurt so much?

But it's too late to change my mind now, too late to take my chances in the Waste once again.

One of the riders presses forward from the circle. This one is dressed differently than the rest, who bear the red tunics with the white house emblem across the front. He's wearing a fine brocade tunic and a long velvet cloak of deep gray. His hair is black touched with silver at the temples and he holds himself with regal bearing, shoulders square, chin up. He has an ethereal grace like the angels. Beautiful, elongated features, eyes that are cold and clever and cruel.

Vyrin?

"Son of the demon king," he says to Asher, "King Vyrin bids you welcome. I am his chief advisor, Lord Kell. I will escort you to the castle and ready you for your meeting with the king."

So, not Vyrin, then. Next to me, Asher nods, jaw tight. "Thank you, Lord Kell."

"I see you have brought your own advisor," Lord Kell says, flicking his gaze to me for the briefest of moments.

"She is not my advisor," Asher says. "I require her to feed on."

Lord Kell's eyebrows arch ever so slightly. "Naturally. We have several other blood fae in residence at the castle, so should you prefer a little... *variety*, we can arrange that."

My cheeks burn with fury. They're discussing me as if I'm merely a piece of livestock Asher brought along.

"That's kind, but won't be necessary," Asher responds.

"Very well, then. Follow me."

Lord Kell turns his horse and urges it into a canter. We follow, the rest of the riders fanned out in a semi-circle behind us. As we make way for the castle, I can't help but watch the last rays of the sun dance over the waves of the ocean, painting the whole thing vermillion and gold. I'd heard tales of the ocean from the Syreni, but never had I imagined something so vast, an endless stretch of blue to rival the sky.

We cross over a small river and make it to the castle right as the shadows of night claim the land. As we pass beneath the massive portcullis into the courtyard beyond, it feels as if we are walking into the mouth of a hungry monster. A shiver runs through me, and I notice Asher dart his eyes to mine for the merest of moments.

Lord Kell halts in the center of the courtyard and servants approach to take the horses. After we've dismounted, he casts his eyes over us disdainfully. His eyes linger on the scarf around my neck.

"I'll send you to the bath house first. Your journey seems to have been taxing indeed."

He gestures to one of the servants standing off to the side and whispers something in her ear. The servant dashes off across the courtyard, and Lord Kell indicates for us to follow him in another direction. The riders of the bronze horses, now on foot, follow behind us once again. It seems they will be our constant companions to ensure we don't escape. Or perhaps they don't realize we have no magic and are afraid what we could do.

We enter the castle and travel through a maze of stone corridors lit by torches. The furniture and décor is sparse, and I can smell a salty tang to the moist air, which I realize must come from the sea. There are few windows and the ceilings are low. I think of the many cathedrals in Night, with their soaring ceilings and rainbow windows, and I feel an ache in my chest. I have never left my home before, so I've never been able to conceive of missing it.

I really hope I don't die here in this dark, dank place.

The bath house, however, is a vast improvement in setting. It's a huge room with high ceilings and a skylight at the apex which offers a glimpse of starry night. There's a large square pool of steaming water in the center of the room with smaller pools branching off it, hidden in alcoves around the perimeter of the chamber. Instead of torches, there are dozens of glowing candles set on ledges in the wall, or in tall brass holders.

Several people are there already, and I avert my eyes from their naked bodies. As a warrior, I'd had to bath in front of others before, but I'd always tried to go when no one else was there. It was just another opportunity for the others to taunt me for being Kieran's pet, for being different. The irony is that I realize now, after all this time, they were right. Though *pawn* is a more apt word than *pet*.

Lord Kell points to an alcove on the far side of the room. "I sent Yumae ahead to prepare a space for you and assist you with anything you need. When you're done, I'll be back to collect you."

He exits the room, though of course the guards stay flanked around the door. Asher turns to the right and walks along the edge of the pool, passing marble columns that rise to the ceiling. I follow him around the edge of the water. The rising steam almost seems to glow in the light of the candles. I notice the other bathers cast gazes over at us, not bothering to hide their curiosity.

When we reach the far side of the room, Yumae and another woman are there waiting for us by a circular pool in the corner. The ceiling is a bit lower here, and a smaller set of columns encircle the space. It's no more than a dozen feet across. There's a large stone bowl holding a variety of soaps and sponges, and candles flicker in metal holders.

My heart starts to race. The last thing I want right now is to feel exposed and vulnerable in front of Asher, especially with an audience. It's not as if he hasn't seen me naked, hasn't touched every part of me. But that was before, and now nothing is the same. Everything would be easier if I hadn't given in to my desires.

I startle as Yumae touches my shoulder to slide my jacket off. She dips her head in apology. I turn to face her and gesture that I can undress myself, but she just murmurs, "Please, milady. Let me help."

My cheeks heat up, but I nod. She tugs off my tunic, and I hear her breath catch in her chest when she sees the bruises covering my body. The bruises Kieran's guards gave me. And of course, I also have two puncture wounds on my breast from Asher. I don't even want to know the thoughts that must be swirling through her head. She peels off my boots and my pants, taking care with my daggers, which had been returned to me before crossing the rift; a small mercy which saved my life and Asher's. I'm surprised they haven't taken them from me, or Asher's sword from him. She folds each thing and sets them in a neat pile on a ledge near the pool, taking care as if they are the finest of fabrics. Lastly, she unravels the makeshift bandage at my neck, saying nothing as she does.

Cool air slides over my skin as I stand there, completely bare. Yumae takes my hand to guide me to the pool. As I turn, I see the backside of Asher as he descends the steps into the pool. Now it's my breath that catches. I hate how beautiful he is. His brown hair just touching his broad shoulders. His muscular back and waist. And below…He could be a statue of an angel, except he's *far* from it.

Asher crosses the small pool and sinks down into the water, taking a seat on a ledge beneath it. As he pivots, his eyes lock onto mine. I'm at the edge of the steps now, Yumae still holding my hand, but she releases it so I can descend into the water. He stiffens as his eyes rove over my body, no doubt taking in the bruising same as Yumae had. His eyes burn and the muscles in his jaw roll. He opens his mouth as if to say something, but then just closes it again and stares stormily past me.

I walk down the steps, which are made of porous rock, as is the bottom of the pool. But when I step to the right and take a seat on the ledge opposite Asher, I can tell the ledge is made of the same marble as the columns, smooth and slick. The water is delightfully hot and has almost a silky feeling, as if mixed with minerals, and it's a pale blue-green color like a bird's egg.

When I'm seated I close my eyes for a moment, both to

enjoy this rare experience that will likely never occur again in my life, and also because I don't want to look at Asher. But even with my eyes shut I can feel his gaze on my body.

A slight splashing sound pops them open again. Across the pool, the woman assisting Asher is kneeling behind him, pouring water from a silver pitcher over his head to wet his hair. I'm captivated for a moment by the sight of it cascading over him, and I stare since his eyes are closed. But my gaze lingers a moment too long, and he opens them again and catches me watching him.

The woman begins to apply soap next, washing his body with one of the sponges. I feel a strange flicker of emotion which I realize a moment later is envy. An odd possessiveness seeing some other woman touch Asher's nude body. Why do I even care? He is not mine any longer, if he ever truly was. He's engaged to Ellielle, after all. I have no claim on him, body or heart.

Distraction comes in the form of Yumae starting the same process for me. She wets my hair with water from the pitcher, then pours soap from a glass bottle, something bright blue in color, and begins to massage it into my scalp. Since my hair is quite long, she runs her hands down the length of it, then piles it up and scrubs everything on top of my head. It feels both luxurious and silly at the same time. I've never had someone bathe me before.

Asher, however, does not seem to find it silly. His eyes lock onto mine, clearly feeling no aversion to doing so as I had. Hunger burns there, but it's not the same wild animal look he has when he craves my blood. I have the urge to look away from the intensity of it, but I hold my head high and meet his gaze full on. He's the one who rejected me. Now he has to endure that decision.

Yumae finishes with my hair and begins to sponge the rest of my body, lathering soap along my shoulders and arms. She takes care to be gentle over the wounds on my neck. When she slides the soapy sponge down over my breasts, Asher stiffens, and a low growl vibrates his body. It's not so much a sound as a sensation that passes through the water to me. Yumae doesn't seem to notice, carrying on with her work.

A few minutes later we're done, and I'm feeling more clean than I've ever felt in my whole life. Strange treatment, given we're in the castle of the man who is supposedly our deadliest enemy. Perhaps Asher is wrong about things. It's been more than two centuries, after all. People can change. He had, after all, I'd seen in it the vision he showed me down in the catacombs.

Yumae and the other servant give us clean velvety robes to wear, and then they escort us back to the door. Lord Kell is already there, and I wonder when he'd returned, and how long he'd been watching.

His eyes rove over us and I suppress a shiver. "I trust you are feeling refreshed. I'll take you to the tailor now to be fitted for new attire."

"Surely you can launder the clothes we wore?" Asher asks, his voice a low rumble.

Kell nods. "Yes, but that attire is not fitting for the ball."

"The ball?" I ask.

"Oh, yes," Kell responds. "King Vyrin is throwing a ball in your honor. It is sure to be a night you'll never forget."

TWELVE

ASHER

I suppress a growl. A ball? It's ludicrous. Vyrin is taking this game even further than I imagined. Toying with me like a cat with a sparrow.

It's beyond infuriating.

Fate is cruel to strip me of my power right before I face my greatest enemy. If I had the wild magic of Night, I would tear this entire castle to the ground, Vyrin along with it.

"When will we meet with Vyrin for negotiations?" I ask, not able to mask the impatience in my voice.

Lord Kell casts me an imperious look. "You will meet the king at the ball, naturally. As for when he chooses to discuss the business between our two realms, I cannot say. In the meanwhile, enjoy our hospitality."

There's a note of malice in his tone on the last sentence, an unspoken *while you still can*.

Without explaining further, he turns on his heel and

leads us back out into the hallway. We travel through the massive castle for several minutes until we arrive in a room that must be the tailor's workspace. There are several cushioned chairs dotted through, along with ornate mirrors along the walls and racks of fine cloth, velvet, brocade, and silk in an array of colors that pop against the gray of the stone.

An older man and woman call greetings to Lord Kell and he leaves us with them, shutting the door as he goes. I can hear the booted footsteps of the guards outside, however. We are not truly alone.

"Come with me," the man says, gesturing for me to follow.

He's wearing a canvas apron with several pockets, scissors and string and scraps of fabric erupting from within. His bushy white eyebrows seem as if they're trying to escape his forehead in a similar fashion. He leads me into a smaller room off the main one, and I notice the woman taking Zara into a room across from mine. The door closes, blocking her from my sight.

I feel a surge of anxiety not being able to keep eyes on her, especially after I saw the bruises on her body in the bathing hall. I'd wanted to ask who did that to her, but I couldn't trust the servants not to share our conversation. I have no doubt that part of all this excessive build-up to the meeting with Vyrin is to gain intel from us. But mostly, it's imperative I don't let on who Zara is to me. If Vyrin thinks she means anything to me at all, he'll make things bad for her just to torture me.

I don't want her dragged into a centuries-old feud that has nothing to do with her. If I know she's safe, I don't care what they do to me. I've known my life was forfeit from the moment those riders came through the rift. It should be easy—since there is nothing between me and Zara anymore, there isn't anything for Vyrin to find out.

Willing myself to relax, I remind myself it's unlikely the tailor is going to mishandle Zara. I force myself to pay attention to the thin, frazzled man who is now taking my measurements with an implement from one of his many pockets. When he's finished, he disappears into a huge closet. Through the gap in the door, I can see him rifling through clothing that hangs from racks inside. A short while later he emerges with a pair of pants, a tunic, and a jacket.

He's apparently been given instructions for what type of outfit I am to wear, because he doesn't ask me my pref-erence on anything. He barely speaks as he makes several quick modifications to the outfit he brought out, sitting at a table a few feet away. When he's done, he has me try it on and looks me up and down.

"Yes," is all he says.

I look like I'm fitted for battle rather than a ball, though there are a few decorative embellishments. The pants are black leather, the tunic pale cream with golden thread stitched along the collar and down the V in the middle. The jacket is also leather, form fitting with small obsidian studs at the cuffs.

"One more thing," the tailor says, and he goes back

into the closet and returns with a pair of boots that travel nearly to my knee. When I put them on, he nods and says, "Good."

We exit the side room, but the door is still shut on Zara's side of the main room.

"They will be a while," the tailor says, though how he knows this, I am unsure.

"I can wait."

I take a seat in one of the chairs in the main room, but a short time later, Lord Kell opens the door and gestures for me to come out. "I'll take you for some refreshments while you wait on your... *companion*."

"That won't be necessary," I respond. "I'm sure you'll have plenty of refreshments at the ball."

"Ahh, but it *is* necessary," Kell says. His dark eyes glitter dangerously. "You being a blood fae, we can't have you arriving hungry to an event with hundreds of guests."

I stiffen, both at being called fae, and at Kell's clear desire to separate me from Zara. If I protest, it will imply she means something to me. Which is no doubt what they're trying to ascertain. "You're too kind," I say, managing to keep my tone neutral, though inside I'm fuming.

Lord Kell smiles a thin smile and leads me down the hall away from Zara. While I no longer feel the tether of wild magic that connected us before the explosion, it almost feels as if I do. As if the further away from her I get, the more it physically pains me. If they do anything to her while I am gone, they will know regret...

We travel what seems twice the length of the Palace of Night, finally arriving in a large antechamber with several cushioned settees and large pillows scattered throughout. Silks are draped from the walls and candles glow in the corners. It looks like some sort of brothel. Even more so because there are scantily clad women and men draped over the furniture.

"I'll wait for you here," Lord Kell says. He pulls the door shut behind him.

Lord Kell had called me blood fae... Vyrin's supposed claim on Illiare, on our people, is that we all descended from the fae, and so he is our rightful ruler. I've read the tales and histories, and it's said there are many fae courts, just as we have different houses in Night. But in the books I read, it wasn't clear where exactly those courts are located. Was Vyrin banished from the ancestral fae lands? Where are they located, and more importantly, where are the other kings and queens? The idea of more like Vyrin is not a pleasant thought.

I have only ever considered myself Daemonium, though rare in that I am a hybrid of both demon and vampire. For Lord Kell to so casually label me something else entirely makes a fresh wave of anger run through my body. But at the same time there's a nagging curiosity... if there's any truth to their claim, I want to know it. The idea of existing without knowing my true origin chafes at my soul.

The blood servants are watching, however, and no doubt will report on my behavior. So, I put aside my musings and I taste each of them, five in total, so nothing can be said of any particular choice. And also because I am desperately hoping that someone will sustain me other than Zara. That my desire for any blood but hers will return.

But they all taste like dust in my mouth. Every single one.

The more I consume, in fact, the more hungry I become, because they remind me that they are not Zara, and their blood is not her blood. And while they do not seem bothered in the slightest when I bite them, which I strongly suspect is due to being drugged, they are not moved by it, either. They do not melt into me as Zara does, they do not make the same sounds of pleasure.

When I'm finished, I stalk to the door and yank it open, causing Lord Kell to startle. "Did you find that to your satisfaction?" he asks.

"Yes, thank you."

He cocks his head to the side as if trying to determine my truthfulness, but then just says, "Let's move along then. The ball will be starting soon. Your companion will meet us there."

Kell and the guards escort me another great distance. I am fairly certain we are moving in the direction of the ocean. I'm trying to keep a feel for the layout of this place, which isn't easy given its vastness and design. We turn down a long hall, and suddenly the castle is quite transformed. Instead of drab gray stone there is marble the color of fresh cream veined with gold and silver. Ornate columns line the path, and the ceiling is painted with scenes of the ocean.

Rising at the far end of the grand hallway are a set of enormous double doors. They're easily five times my height, and painted gold. Doormen on each side open them soundlessly as we approach, revealing a wide set of steps leading to a huge ballroom. The ceilings here soar even higher, and the far end of the room opens onto an expansive balcony. I can hear waves crashing beyond and see the sparkle of moonlight on the water.

The ball seems in full swing already, despite Kell indicating that I am the guest of honor. Hundreds of people mingle and dance and drink. They are dressed in exquisite gowns and many wear masks over their faces, glimmering things set with gemstones and feathers and pearls. There's a huge table laden with exquisite food, and a fountain on the opposite side of the room shaped like a swan. Golden liquid pours from the swan's beak, and giggling guests dance by, filling crystal goblets with the stuff. A trio of harpists play in one corner.

I'm trying to absorb the splendor of it all when Lord Kell clears his throat behind me. "Your companion has arrived."

I turn from my position at the apex of the steps, and my breath leaves my chest.

Zara approaches, a half dozen guards behind her. She's wearing an emerald-green dress that cascades to the floor, voluminous and set with tiny gemstones. It has no straps, hugging tightly to her breasts, revealing her bare shoulders and arms. The color glows against her bronze skin and raven hair, which someone has pinned atop her head with an array of jeweled clips. They seem to have somehow masked her bruises. She looks exquisite, and I hate the storm of emotions that burns in my chest.

I offer her my arm, because there's no way in hell I'm letting her walk through this crowd of vipers unescorted. No doubt I'm not the only one who will notice how delectable she is. Her eyes flick to mine, then she takes a quick glance down at my outfit. She fidgets slightly, clearly uncomfortable in her attire.

"They took my daggers," she whispers as she loops her arm through mine.

Of course that's what she's thinking about.

My lips quirk into a smile for a half moment before I can contain myself, and we begin to walk down the marble steps into the melee beyond. It doesn't seem Lord Kell has further instructions for us, as he stays at the top of the stairs with the guards. No one seems to take much notice as we descend toward the crowd, that is, until we reach the last step. When we do, a man turns around, someone I assumed was just a random guest.

I recognize him instantly.

"Greetings, Lord of Night," says King Vyrin. "I'm so happy you could join me."

THIRTEEN

ZARA

A sher goes rigid next to me, and I stare at the man who greeted us. He is tall and built like a warrior, and he looks young, perhaps even a bit younger than Asher. A scar runs down the entire left side of his face, from forehead to jaw passing over his eye, but it doesn't detract from his beauty. His hair is thick and golden, his eyes a startling jade green, and it's there that his age is shown. I can't see the centuries by the lines on his face, but I can read them in his eyes. There are depths upon depths there, and a coldness that makes me shiver.

Vyrin turns his gaze abruptly and stares at me as I am staring at him. "And who might your lovely companion be?" The smile he throws me is charming and predatorial both.

"This is Zara." Asher's voice has lowered several octaves, and the hint of a growl echoes in it. "She is my blood companion."

"Is that so?" Vyrin's eyebrows shoot up and he pivots his gaze back to Asher. "You could have brought anyone in your city to parlay with me, and you brought your dinner?"

Another tremble runs through me, but this time it's anger. I'm getting really tired of being labeled as a food source.

"You've thrown us quite the party," Asher says, waving a hand at the crowd beyond. It's clear he's reined in his reaction and is changing the subject. "I hadn't expected such a warm welcome."

"Well, of course," Vyrin says. His voice is silk and thorns, both alluring and sharp all at once, like everything else about him. "It's been more than two centuries since our great houses have gathered. A celebration was in order. And I trust Lord Kell has been an adequate host?"

"He has," Asher responds. "Most hospitable indeed."

"I told him to make sure you visited our blood servants. They are simply exquisite." Vyrin's eyes have a strange intensity to them, and he flicks his gaze to me. "Have you sampled them yet?"

"I have," Asher says.

The idea of Asher drinking from blood servants makes my stomach tighten. When he drinks from me, it's so... *intimate*. I don't want to think of him experiencing that with anyone else. Even if it's a stupid thought, because Asher doesn't want anything to do with me at all.

"Ahh, lovely." Vyrin's eyes meet mine again. "Though none of them could possibly be as divine as your Zara."

Asher shifts his weight almost as if he's pressing into me. I can feel the heat of his body wrap around mine.

Vyrin gestures toward the room behind him. "Many other tempting delicacies await you beyond. Lots to taste, to *savor*. Pleasure to be had." He finally tears his eyes from mine and levels a blade-edged smile at Asher. "Please, go forth and enjoy. You and I shall discuss matters later."

"I'm looking forward to it," Asher says with a tight-lipped smile.

He leads me forward as Vyrin melts back into the crowd, almost as if he'd vanished. I suck in a breath, not realizing I hadn't drawn a lungful of air since Vyrin approached us.

Asher leads us toward the table heaped high with food, but as we approach, he whispers, "Do not eat or drink anything here."

"Why?" I ask, glancing up at him.

"It is never wise to partake of anything a fae offers you. Most especially this fae, and most especially this ball."

"Well, you apparently got to feed earlier, whereas I have had nothing since dawn," I snap. "How long do you expect me to go without food or water?"

Asher's jaw rolls in agitation. "We have other *much* more important matters at play than your next meal."

I growl and try to pull away from him, but he locks his arm over mine so I can't move. "You are not leaving my side, Zara."

"So now you suddenly want my company?"

"I *don't* want it," Asher says. "But it is very much not safe for you here. You have no idea what you've walked into."

"I can handle myself, magic or no magic."

"You've never experienced anything like Vyrin in your wildest dreams," Asher snarls. "Don't be stubborn."

"And don't be condescending." I level a glare at him, which he ignores.

Asher grabs a golden plate and begins to add things to it. "They're watching us, so we need to pretend we're going along with everything."

I grab my own plate and do the same, though my stomach rumbles hungrily at all the luscious things I can't partake of. It's true what I said to Asher—I can't starve myself forever. But I can wait a little bit longer. And hope against hope that we get out of here before I gnaw my own arm off.

After we fill our plates we stroll throughout the crowd, pretending to take bites of our food. My eyes rove over the opulence of the room. Everything is ornate, dripping with decadence. Even the air is perfumed, a cloyingly sweet scent like flowers. My irritation with Asher slowly dissolves. I know we need to stick together, and I suppose his sudden desire to protect me is better than trying to get as far away from me as possible. We visit the swan pouring golden liquid, which upon closer inspection smells like honey. The urge to taste it is almost overwhelming, as if it's enchanted.

It's strange, though, because I've felt almost no magic since we crossed into Cyrena. Is it because I've lost my own connection to magic, or because the magic here feels different than what I'm used to? I'd expected Vyrin himself to possess a great deal of it, since he's ruled for so long, but even he seemed to hold only a faint spark of anything I could sense.

As we move through the crowd, pretending to nibble at our food and sip the golden wine, the other guests seem to take no notice of us, as if we're invisible. It's a bit unsettling, though better than the alternative. We deposit our plates and goblets on a small table, and I suddenly have the strangest sense as if I've lost track of time. It seems simultaneously that we just arrived, and also that we've been here milling about for hours.

"We should dance," Asher says abruptly.

Surprise ripples along my skin. I could no sooner have guessed that the Lord of Night would ask me to dance than I could predict how many falling stars would move across the sky tonight. "Dance?"

He nods. "Everyone else is dancing. It will be noticed if we don't participate."

I go rigid as he tugs me toward the end of the room closest to the ocean, where it seems over a hundred people are spinning and cavorting on the floor.

"I am a spy and a recluse. Do you really think I know how to dance?" I stare at him scornfully, crossing my arms over my chest.

"You've *never* danced?" Asher asks. "Not once?"

I shake my head.

Something changes in his eyes, a softening, a stir of emotion like the melancholy song of the waves beyond. "We will likely die in this place," he says, reaching for my hand. "You cannot leave this world without at least once having danced."

My eyebrows arch. "And you, the most feared and dreaded man in the City of Night, are going to teach me to dance?"

Asher smiles for a moment, and then he pulls me hard against him. "I have seen you fight, shadow assassin. Dancing will be child's play for one such as you."

My heart pounds as I find myself suddenly in the curve of his arms. I can feel the warmth of his muscles against mine, smell the leather of his pants and jacket mingled with his own natural scent. What I don't want, if we're really going to die here, is to die without Asher's forgiveness.

He winds the fingers of one hand into mine and leads me off into the crowd. We stay near the edge, not wanting to get stuck deep within the throng of bodies toward the center of the floor. The music from the nearby harpists curls around us, and a breeze from the ocean carries the scent of salt and rain and far-off lands. I'd been trapped behind the Waste for so long, never thinking I'd live to see the world beyond. Only ever imagining it, wondering what lay on the other side of my prison walls. And now, in an odd and unfortunate twist of fate, I am out in the midst of it, in all its deadly beauty.

Asher's earth-colored eyes hold mine, as do his hands, one intertwined in my fingers, the other wrapped around the small of my back. We spin, and I do not think about what happened between us. And I do not think about what lies ahead. There is just this moment and the next and the next, the dance and the sea and the music spiraling around us.

I blink and realize we've somehow been swept deep into the midst of the dancers. I don't remember how we got here. Had we moved, or had they? Bodies crush in around us, and I can smell their sweat and the wine they spilled on their skin. Most of the dancers wear masks, some beautiful, some dark and grotesque. I feel light-headed and the room spins slightly.

"Zara," Asher says, both his tone and his eyes serious, but he doesn't have a chance to finish the sentence.

"There you are," Vyrin says. "I simply must steal a dance with this vision."

And suddenly my hand is in his instead of Asher's, and we're spinning away. I whip my head around, but I only catch a flash of Asher before he is lost in the crowd.

"What are you doing?" I ask, shaking my head. It's beginning to buzz unpleasantly as if I've had too much of the golden wine. Except I've had none.

"Dancing, my shadow witch, just dancing."

Vyrin spins me, and for several long moments, all I see is color and sparkling lights and the distant glimmer of the moon on the waves.

Through the fog of my thoughts, his words finally sink in. "Shadow witch? Why did you call me that?"

Vyrin shoots me a smile, revealing fangs like a wolf. Or was that someone sliding past us on the dance floor with a wicked mask? Everything is moving so fast.

"It's what you are, isn't it?" Those jade eyes burn into me, as if peering into my soul. "We both know you're not just a blood donor for the demon lord."

I feel both alarmed and strangely pleased that someone finally sees me for what I am. But I don't trust this fae king, so I bite my tongue.

"I could sense the residue of magic on you the moment I laid eyes on you, Zara," Vyrin says. "You sparkle with it as if your very bones are made of the stuff. Your blood and your soul."

"My… my soul?"

I blink. The face of a bat spins past, the wings of a butterfly. It seems as if I can see the notes of music from the harpists hanging in the air, dancing along with the rest of us.

"You are like *him*," Vyrin continues. "It's no wonder he won't let you out of his sight. He needs you, though I'll bet he doesn't admit it, does he?"

I nod my head without even thinking, as if a puppet pulled on strings. "No—I mean, it's not like that," I stammer. What is wrong with me?

"You both lost it, though, your magic… how did that happen?" His eyes are sharp on mine, yet he's smiling in that charming way. Charming as a jackal…

"We... the explosion..."

We're spinning, the room is spinning, the night is spinning.

"No!" I yell, but it sounds garbled, distant.

I shove away from Vyrin.

Something is very wrong with this place. I push toward the balcony, toward the fresh air coming off the water. I need to get away from him, from this crowd.

When I hit the banister at the edge of the balcony, I almost topple over it. Everything spins and my heart lurches in my chest. The ocean rushes up to meet me, the stars wheel overhead. And then I feel the cool stone gripped beneath my fingers, and it brings me back just enough to sink to my knees so I don't fall over the edge. I sit and take big, gasping gulps of air, trying to calm down.

I'm still sitting there when Asher strides up.

"Zara! Are you okay?" He looks frantic and furious both, staring down at me on the stone tiles of the balcony.

"No..." I murmur, shaking my head. "Don't you feel it?"

He nods, expression stern. "This is what I was afraid of. Vyrin is ancient, and the fae are known for their trickery..."

He stops mid-sentence as the subject of conversation saunters out onto the balcony to join us. "Are you feeling quite alright, dear?" Vyrin asks, grinning down at me. "Too much wine?"

Asher bristles and pulls me to my feet.

"I have just the thing for you two," Vyrin continues.

"The blood fae are having a little private party over in one of the antechambers... you must join the fun."

"Zara's not feeling up to more fun right at the moment," Asher grinds out between clenched teeth.

"Nonsense," Vyrin says with his wicked smile. "The night is young. I *insist*."

FOURTEEN

ASHER

Vyrin grabs for Zara's hand, as he had on the dance floor. But my head has cleared now, and whatever was muddling it before has passed. I step between him and Zara and pull her against me.

I'm imagining how it will feel to pull Vyrin apart slowly, limb by limb.

It's clear he's taken an interest in Zara, despite my attempts to downplay her importance. Which is exactly why I didn't want anyone coming along on this journey with me. Most especially not Zara. I may not have a future with her, but I will protect her with my life. Which means I can't go down like a martyr in this place, because that will leave her at Vyrin's mercy.

I may have lost my magic and my city both, but I will *not* fail in this regard. I will see Zara safely back to Night, even if it takes my last breath.

But I'll play Vyrin's little game. For now.

"Lead the way," I say to him with a tight smile.

Vyrin's grin only widens, and he moves off through the crowd. I look down at Zara and nod ever so slightly, hoping I can portray some of what I'm thinking in that small gesture. She walks at my side as we weave through the partygoers, following the fae king to whatever devilry he has planned next.

As we travel back through the room, I notice that things are devolving rather quickly. It seems just minutes ago we were dancing, and people were eating and drinking and talking. Now there are people clustered together in various states of undress. I see a woman pressed up against a marble column, a man on his knees before her, face buried between her legs as another woman kisses her neck and sucks on her earlobe. Across the room a woman is bent over one of the food tables, her upper body crushing a tray of red fruit as a man with stag horns thrusts into her from behind. In the swan fountain, a half dozen people writhe in the pool of sparkling wine, their moans and the sound of skin slapping skin cutting the air.

Zara's body is tight as a bowstring as we pass through the crowd. Vyrin guides us into a far corner of the room, back behind the elaborate staircase we'd come down. It seems hours ago at this point, though it can't possibly have been that long. Can it?

In the alcove beneath the stairs the lighting is dim, punctuated by lanterns which hang on hooks around the perimeter. There are several velvet settees, and a dozen people are already crowded on them, spilling over onto cushions and fur rugs on the floor. The smell of blood hits me like a hammer, and a wave of hunger moves through me. Without meaning to, my grip tightens on Zara.

"Please, join your kind, relax and enjoy," Vyrin says, gesturing for us to join the others.

There's a small spot at the end of one of the armless settees, so I lead us over to it. Zara's eyes meet mine questioningly as I sit down. It's not big enough for both of us, so I pull her down into my lap. I wish I could talk to her in private. Explain that if we play Vyrin's game a bit longer, we may get out of this evening unscathed.

But I can't say what I want to say out loud. Luckily, I don't have to. Zara must understand, because she just looks at me, and then slowly turns her head to one side so I have access to her neck. A growl rumbles through my chest unbidden. I don't want to feed on her in front of all these people, let alone Vyrin. But I know I have to. Not only to keep Vyrin at bay, but because my hunger is leaving me little choice.

I want Zara so deeply it hurts.

My left hand slides into her hair, fisting the silky strands at the back of her head, and my right wraps around her waist. When I press my lips to the soft skin of her neck, she lets out a little sigh, barely audible. I can feel Vyrin's gaze, heavy on us both, a leering voyeur as my teeth slide out. But I can't keep my inner beast in check any longer.

When I bite Zara, she shudders against me. I can tell she's trying to hold it in, and by the muffled sound she makes, it's clear she's biting her own lip to keep from crying out. For some reason this drives me even more wild. We couldn't be in more danger than right now, in this palace, with this wicked and twisted king watching our every move, but all I want to do is throw Zara down on the fur rug at my feet and enter her in every possible way.

She is more dangerous than all the fae combined.

Why does she hold this power over me?

Her blood rushes into my mouth, intoxicating as always. Where my arm wraps across the front of her body, I can feel one of her breasts, and how her nipple hardens against me. I let out another growl, and this time she can't suppress the moan that ripples up from her throat. Everything else falls away, and Zara consumes my existence. My reality is her skin, her hair, her essence. The sound of her breathing and the smell of her body reacting to mine.

When she suddenly shrieks and jerks back, I pull away from her neck, my senses shifting from pleasure to danger in an instant.

The man sitting next to us on the settee has his teeth embedded in Zara's wrist, drinking from her. We'd been so wrapped up in each other that I hadn't even sensed him turning around. Rage roars through me, and I shove the man off of Zara so hard that he tumbles onto the floor. Standing, I encircle her with both arms, my eyes promising death to any who approach us.

Laughter cuts through the red haze of my fury. Vyrin makes a placating gesture. "Calm down, Asher. We all share here in the blood den."

"I. Do not. Share." Each of my words cuts like an axe.

Zara is bleeding freely from her wrist, and the expression she levels on the man who bit her is enough to send him scurrying from the room.

"I think your little blood servant can take care of herself," Vyrin says jovially. "Sit back down. Enjoy the festivities."

"We had an arduous journey today," I growl. "I trust our gracious host will show us to our room now."

Vyrin pauses for several heavy heartbeats, his jade eyes burning into mine, and then he inclines his head. "Of course. You are my honored guests."

Lord Kell appears abruptly at the edge of the room, as if he'd been following us all along. Which he probably had. He makes a small gesture, expression impassive, and we follow him back up the stairs. As we walk, I pull off my leather jacket and wrap it around Zara's arm, cradling it against her body with one hand as my other wraps protectively around her shoulder.

We travel to the floor above us, where Lord Kell opens a door onto a large room with a balcony overlooking the sea. "These are your quarters for the night. There's a servant stationed at the end of the hall should you require anything." He gives us one last dismissive look, then strides back down the hall.

As soon as he's gone, I shut the door behind us and bolt it. Not that it will do much good if Vyrin decides to break it down later. I turn to Zara, shaking with fury as my pent-up emotions rise to the surface. "Are you okay?"

She nods, lips drawn tight, jaw clenched. "I'm fine. It surprised me is all."

I place my hands on the outsides of her biceps. "I will kill every single one of them. I promise you."

Zara cocks her head to the side slightly. "As long as you leave some for me."

The look on her face is fierce and deadly, a goddess of carnage and wrath. I realize my hands are still gripping her bare arms. It's an intimate touch, something I shouldn't really be doing since she's not mine anymore. And I'd forgotten for a short time that she never really was.

I spin and begin to pace the room, a storm of emotions brewing inside me. It's luxurious, like the ballroom below. I'm surprised they haven't housed us in the more spartan side of the castle. The floors are pale marble, a seafoam green, and the walls are painted with murals of seaside villages and ships riding waves, beset by sirens and kraken. The crown moldings are painted a pale gold, and the ceiling is set with mirrors of various sizes and shapes, circles and seashells and waves.

My feet lead me to the balcony, where the dark of the night and the chill of the air help settle my nerves. The ocean is beautiful, but I want nothing more than to be back in my home. Night is an empty hole in my heart, even as war-torn and fraught with peril as it is. I stand there, wind tousling my hair and raising goosebumps along my skin.

"Don't turn around," Zara calls softly. "I have to get out of this hideous dress."

I should tell her that the dress, and her in it, is far from hideous, but I bite my tongue. It's not my place. And it doesn't matter anymore.

My mind begins to turn over images of her taking it off. The fact that she told me not to turn around just makes me want to do it all the more. What does she even have to put on in its place? I think I'd seen a wardrobe when we entered, up against the far wall. Whether or not it has clothes that fit us remains to be seen.

What seems like an eternity later, she says, "Okay."

I wait, not wanting to seem too eager to turn around. When I finally do, I see she's wearing an oversized white tunic, likely made for a man. It has short sleeves, a V-neck, and hangs about halfway down her thighs. I raise my brows.

Zara shrugs. "It's the only suitable thing in the wardrobe. The others were…."

She trails off, and the way she says it makes me wonder what exactly is in that wardrobe. But Zara doesn't need anything special. The way the tunic barely covers her long legs, the cascade of her raven hair down her back… I'm suddenly very aware of the fact that we're alone in this room with only one bed. I once again wonder at the cruel irony of my recent fate.

I realize I'm staring, and it's not missed on Zara, either. She locks eyes with me and shifts her balance slightly as if readying for an attack. Instinct, no doubt, because my inner demon is bursting at the seams. She can feel the predator within, she's a trained warrior, after all. I wrestle my blood lust down, letting out a breath to break the tension between us.

Zara's shoulders relax slightly. "So, what's our plan?"

I grind my teeth together. I wish I had one. Without magic, even with our fighting skills we're going to have a hard time—impossible, really—getting out of this fortress alive. I feel trapped, hopeless.

But I'm going to find a way out of here. I will *not* fail.

"For tonight, we rest. Tomorrow, we meet with Vyrin, find out what he wants. If it's something more than merely to toy with me. Then we figure out an escape plan."

"You don't think it'll be too late then?" Zara's eyes hold mine, two violet flames.

"Whatever he's up to, he's going to take his time with it." I point to the room around us. "Putting us up in one of his best rooms. The bathing hall, the feast. He's making a big show of us being guests here. Enjoying himself far too much to cut our throats tomorrow."

Zara shivers. "So, he's not done yet."

"Not by far." I sigh and run a hand through my hair. "I fear he's just getting started."

A sher's expression is so serious that another shiver crawls across my skin. Everything tonight at the ball confirmed what he'd warned me of in the rift: Vyrin is a sadistic ruler who clearly enjoys throwing his power around. I've lived my entire life in a war zone, spying and stealing and fighting. But this deadly game we now find ourselves in is more dangerous than everything in my past combined.

I don't see how we can possibly escape alive.

"I—I think Vyrin may have taken an interest in me," I say quietly. "He doesn't believe I'm just your… blood servant."

Asher stiffens. "I noticed."

"He said he could smell the magic on me," I continue. "But he can also tell that we lost it."

A string of curses from across the room. Asher begins

to pace. "I was hoping to avoid him finding out about that. And that you're not my blood servant."

"Well… that part is mostly true." I raise my chin and meet his gaze when he pivots toward me. "Ellielle sent me along for that exact reason."

"She sent you along to get rid of you," he growls.

"Well, it seems she'll get her wish."

Asher looks murderous. "That's not going to happen."

I know I should just go along with Asher's newfound sense of honor and protection. It's the wise thing to do—we're in the castle of our greatest enemy, and to be united is to be stronger. But it's so opposite his cold fury of just hours before that my emotions can't stop reeling. Confusion being key among them.

So maybe it's because we're far from home and likely going to die here that I let the words pour out of my mouth.

"But don't you share Ellielle's wishes? To be rid of me? I thought you *hated* me. I thought you never wanted to see me again."

Asher stops his pacing, my words hitting him as he's walking away from me. He turns abruptly, the look on his face so furious that I take a step backward.

It's several long moments before he speaks.

"You betrayed me." His words are low and deadly, shaking my bones. "You lied about everything. And I *do* hate what you did."

He stalks toward me, a rolling storm front. He stops an

inch from my chest, his eyes burning into mine with such intensity it feels like staring into the sun.

"But my feelings for you were not manufactured, as *yours* were, so I can't just be rid of them. Though I wish with every ounce of my being that I could." His jaw rolls and his eyes flash. "I wish I could forget everything about you, Zara."

"How *dare you*," I growl. I place my hands on his chest and try to shove him away from me, which is akin to trying to shove a mountain. He barely moves. "Do not attempt to define my feelings or the truth behind them. I told you what happened, the lies I was told by Kieran. How could I have known the truth before I met you? Before I realized the connection to Night that we share?"

"And how could we ever have a future when Kieran had you first?" Asher snarls.

"Kieran never *had* me, not in the way you imply," I snap. "Kieran never even saw me in a night shirt like this, let alone wearing nothing at all. He was my mentor because I had no one else. He manipulated me, used me as a pawn, yes. But he wasn't strong enough to be with me in the way that you were. My magic would have *destroyed* him."

Asher steps even closer, anger roiling off of him. "You are a liar, a spy, a thief, and an assassin. How could I ever trust you?"

I glare back at him. "And you are a murderer, the most dreaded and hated man in all of Night. You consume blood and souls, and you unleashed the wild magic that demolished our city. It is *beyond* hypocrisy for you to judge my actions."

"No one has ever spoken to me that way in my entire life," Asher growls, his inner demon roiling just below the surface.

"Well then, it's clearly long overdue."

Asher doesn't respond verbally, he just growls again and picks me up, lifting me by my ass cheeks and carrying me the three strides to the bed behind us. When he reaches it, he doesn't toss me down as I'd expected. Instead, he pins me against one of the tall, wooden posts at the foot of the bed. He locks gazes with me for a long moment, a look so ablaze with emotion that my breath leaves my body.

Then, slowly, he slides one hand up my thigh.

His eyes don't leave mine as the tip of one finger grazes my opening. His fingers on my skin feel like comets, and another sigh rushes out of me. The post of the bed presses into my back, and Asher's thighs are crushed against mine.

He teases at the entrance to my sweet core, his voice low and gravelly. "I *am* a villain and a monster..."

A moan works its way up my throat. My heart is racing so fast it hurts.

Asher leans in, lips at my earlobe, breath hot against my neck. "But I think you want this anyways."

I nod slowly, but he shakes his head.

"*Say it.* If you want me, you have to say it this time."

The desire for him to enter me is making my vision spotty. Need and longing throb through my core. Before, when we'd been together, I'd thought it was just the wild magic drawing us together, a fight I couldn't win, Night being so much stronger than the two of us.

But our magic is gone now, and this craving is burning me up just the same.

Asher swirls his fingertip inside me and I cry out. "Yes! I want this."

He plunges his finger deep inside of me and the room spins with stars. His free hand weaves into the hair at the base of my neck as he presses even closer into me. "Want what, Zara?"

His finger slides back out and I shudder. "I want *you*," I whisper.

I can feel the hard length of him pressed against my body, and at my words he grows even harder. He thrusts his finger back into me, curling it inside and swirling it in a way that makes my knees buckle. But he holds me upright as he gyrates his finger in and out of me.

"Only me?" he asks, breath warm against my earlobe, his teeth grazing against it.

His thumb is rolling over my clit as he continues to drive his long finger in and out of me, and the world is spinning away into an ocean of pleasure. I can hear the waves outside beyond the balcony, and it feels like I'm being carried away into them.

"Only you, Asher," I gasp. "You know it's only you."

He growls and the vibration of it in my ear pushes me over the edge. As I begin to convulse and cry out, he speeds up the pulsing of his finger and I am lost to ecstasy.

This time when Asher lifts me, he does toss me on the bed, not waiting for me to recover from my intense climax. He stands at the edge, pulling his shirt off over his head in one swift movement. His eyes devour me as he whips his belt off and steps out of his pants, revealing the huge length of him. I shiver as he bends over me, his hands going to the V of my night shirt. He rips it right down the middle, and the pieces of it flutter to each side.

"This does not mean I forgive you," he says, and then he thrusts inside me.

I cry out as the length of him fills me. My fingers dig into his back and I wrap my legs around him as he rolls his hips, pulling back and entering me again. Asher is not gentle, and neither am I. He growls and lets out a moan of pain and pleasure as my nails cut into the backs of his shoulder blades, and he thrusts harder into me. I rock my hips up to meet him as we crash together, in and out, faster and faster.

A strange buzz of energy builds between us. My head is still fuzzy from my release a few minutes before, and now the room grows hazy, heat flaming off of us, as if we might actually catch fire. The pleasure is growing in waves again, sucking me toward an inexorable release. With each thrust, it feels like Asher and I are dissolving into each other, melding into one. I can feel his anger and his passion, his hunger and his need. And I can feel my own, swirling around his like we're two moons colliding.

Abruptly, Asher rolls me into an upright position so I'm straddling his lap. Our chests press together and his eyes burn into mine. I wrap my arms around his neck and roll my hips, grinding into him, moving up and down along the length of his cock. The fingers of one hand twist into his hair. He holds my hips tightly, digging his fingers into me as I move.

When he kisses up the side of my neck, I shudder and let out a whimper.

"Not yet," he growls. "You *will* wait for me, Zara."

His teeth graze my soft skin, and then they plunge into me.

Bliss unfolds within me and I bite my lip to keep from going over the edge, so hard I can taste my own blood. Feeling the hard length of Asher inside my core while his teeth penetrate me at the same time is too much. Despite his directive, I'm not going to be able to hold on much longer. Ecstasy is burning through me, and that same strange buzz is getting stronger and stronger. A pressure building, separate from the pleasure of our physicality.

Asher sucks at my neck, his lips tight on my skin. His arms slide up to wrap around my back, crushing me closer to him. I feel him start to shake as I pulse my hips faster, feel his fingers tighten, bruising my skin where they dig into me. A cry rips from my throat as the first wave of my climax hits me. Pleasure blossoms in my center and radiates from where Asher's teeth have punctured me.

He releases my neck and his lips find mine, his tongue claiming my mouth. Another moan ripples through me, vibrating between us. He probes me hard as if tasting my desire, then he pulls back, letting out a yell and driving his hips up into me as he releases. His final thrust sends me spinning over the crystalline edge of ecstasy, wave after wave of it rolling through me as I collapse against him, convulsing and crying out.

As I cling to Asher, feeling as if I've been utterly destroyed and brought back to life again, I realize that there's something else shimmering between us, hanging between the sheen of sweat on our bodies and the lingering pleasure.

My heart goes still.

"I can feel my magic," I whisper.

CHAPTER
SIXTEEN
ASHER

As I hold Zara in my arms, I forget momentarily that she betrayed me, that there is no future between us. None of that exists, and she is just this shimmering, delicate creature who speaks to my soul in a way no one else ever has.

"I can feel my magic," she says, her words warm against the skin of my neck where we cling to each other.

And I realize, in the stillness between us, that I can feel mine, too.

It's very faint, nothing like the immense force of Night that, until very recently, thrummed inside of me, a storm always on the verge of breaking loose. No, this is a fragile feeling, a soft glow in my chest. The barest, glittering hope.

"I feel it, too," I murmur.

Zara straightens slightly, meeting my eyes. "Do you think..."

She trails off, and I shake my head as reality comes crashing in around me. I slide my hands down to her hips and lift her off of me, setting her on the bed and getting up.

If Zara and I joining together is the key to our magic returning…

Is it a temporary thing, until the full strength of our magic returns? Or does this mean I'm bonded to her forever? Just a few days ago I would have wanted nothing more, but now that I know who she really is, nothing is the same. It *can't* be.

"Asher," she says softly.

"I need time to think," I growl, stalking out onto the balcony.

I stand there, in the darkness and the cold sea air, my thoughts spinning for an interminable length of time. The magic spinning within me is so meager that I don't dare try to summon it. But even as weak as it is, I feel something else now, too. A line of connection to Night, like the thinnest gossamer strand of a spider's web, stretching from my solar plexus eastward toward my home. What is happening there in my absence? Is the city collapsing deeper and deeper into chaos as the wild magic runs rampant? How many lives have been lost?

There is another connection I feel, another delicate strand. That one leads directly behind me.

When I finally turn back around, probably an hour later, Zara is asleep on the bed. I watch her from afar, her features soft in sleep, not sharp and fierce as they are when she's awake. I try to imagine her as a child, growing up with the Animus, living under my brother's burning hatred of me. Her sister taken from her, Kieran painting me as the target for her revenge.

I understand why she did what she did.

Even so, I don't know how we can have a future together.

Exhausted, I walk to the small settee in the corner of the room and lay down on it. Sleep claims me moments after I close my eyes.

It seems only moments later that a hammering sound breaks through my dreams. As I try to claw my way to wakefulness, the sound grows louder, more incessant.

When I finally manage to sit up, Zara is already standing at the edge of the bed, a sheet wrapped around her. Her eyes dart between me and the door. An understanding passes between us: we can either answer it, or it will be broken down.

She turns for the door. I stand and follow her, pulling my pants on and catching up to her right as she reaches it. Her eyes flick to mine once more as she reaches out and unbolts it, then pulls it open. Lord Kell is standing there with a dozen guards.

"The king requests an audience," he says, no emotion on his face.

"In the middle of the night?" Zara asks, her tone blade-edged.

Kell gestures behind us. I flick my gaze over my shoulder, where the slightest edge of red can be seen on the horizon.

"Ahh," I say, not bothering to keep the sarcasm from my tone. "Well then, perfectly reasonable. A few moments to get dressed?"

Kell nods sharply.

We close the door again and hurriedly prepare ourselves. Our clothes from the day before had been laundered and placed in the wardrobe, so at least we have something comfortable to wear again, unlike the forced finery for the ball. Zara looks herself again in her form-fitting pants, jacket, and boots, though lacking her daggers. I don my pants, tunic, cloak, and boots also. When we step out into the hall again, Kell turns without a word and the guards file in behind us as we are escorted to the king.

It doesn't take long to reach the throne room. As we enter, my eyes skim down the length of the enormous room and rest on the man who summoned us here, though it's such a long distance I can't make out much of him yet. The room is the size of two large cathedrals back-to-back. Similarly, the ceiling soars overhead, arched and ornate. Angels and demons and strange, twisted woodland beasts are carved into the gray stone along the moldings and fluted pillars supporting the roof. Flaming candelabra line the walls, and stationed between them in intervals, every dozen feet or so, stands a heavily armed guard.

When we draw closer, I can see that Vyrin sits in a massive throne made of some dark metal that looks like it came from the sky. It is ornately wrought and set with so many rubies it looks as if it drips blood like a living, beating heart. Vyrin himself is robed in pale gray in a shade that nearly matches the coronet at his brow. His green eyes bore into me as we approach.

"I trust you slept well," he asks as we stop before him. His lips quirk up into the hint of a smile.

Still toying with us, clearly. I nod, jaw tight. We have a chance of getting out of here now that our magic is returning. If we can keep Vyrin entertained a bit longer, we may be able to make our escape. Just a bit longer...

Vyrin shifts in his chair, leaning back, gaze swiveling to Zara. My body goes rigid. I don't care for his attention on her in the slightest.

"And I hope you both enjoyed the festivities last night?" His eyes dip to the puncture wound on Zara's wrist where the blood fae bit her. "I think it fair to say that I am a magnanimous and hospital host, am I not?"

I feel a knot growing in my stomach. There's a manic gleam to Vyrin's eyes that sets my nerves on edge.

"Well, as much as I'd love the celebration to continue, it is time to move on to the reason I summoned you here."

Zara's shoulder brushes against mine where she stands next to me, and I can feel the tension running through her body, too. I'd told her last night that we had more time to plan an escape. I have the sick feeling that I'm about to be proven very, very wrong.

"For over two centuries, our people have been cut off from each other. That waste that encircles your city is the perfect defense, I must say." Here Vyrin's eyes burn even brighter. "A way to keep precious resources inside, and keep everyone and everything else out. Especially when you don't want the outside world to take back what you stole. To seek revenge for treason of the highest order."

I go still, my blood slowing in my veins. "Of what do you speak, Vyrin?"

"I speak, son of the demon king," Vyrin snarls, "Of your theft of all the magic in Aureon."

SEVENTEEN

ZARA

I flinch away from the fae king as his words hit me.

Theft of all the magic in Aureon?

My mind spins. Does that mean the day Asher accidentally unleashed the wild magic that nearly demolished Night, over two hundred years prior, he summoned it from...

Everywhere?

I can't even wrap my head around it.

"It was a nice touch, though insulting, that you tried to hide your magic from me when you came here," Vyrin continues, his sadistic smile back in place. "But I felt it stir last night, and I feel it now, crouching within you."

Horror rises in my throat. He had felt when we...*dark goddess.*

"You have everything wrong," Asher growls, his eyes shooting daggers at the king. "We did not attempt to steal

121

the magic. It was a terrible accident that caused—still causes—great suffering for our people. We had no idea there was a loss of magic beyond our borders."

Vyrin laughs, high-pitched and sharp like broken bottles. "A likely story. One that I do not believe even for a moment."

"But if you don't have magic," I begin, shaking my head, "Then how did you…last night, at the ball. Everything seemed strange."

"Without magic, we have become skilled alchemists," Vyrin responds. "I find that adding a little something to the air makes the ball more exciting for everyone." A grin, revealing teeth that look wrong somehow. Too pointed.

I remember the sweet floral smell in the ballroom, and my eyes widen.

"I swear to you, we are not hiding magic intentionally," Asher says. "If I knew how to give it back, I would."

"Full of altruism, are you?" Vyrin's face twists with anger. "How convenient that when my armies were within days of crushing your father's forces you somehow erect an impenetrable barrier around your city and siphon *all* the power in *all* the realms behind that barrier. It's genius, really. Why would any sane man give it back?" He runs a hand over his face. "You must think me an imbecile. A fool of the highest order."

"I can share the truth, but I cannot force you to accept it," Asher growls.

"*Truth.*" Vyrin pauses for several long moments, a

strangling silence falling across the room like fingers around my throat. "I will share my truth now," he finally says.

"Last night, while you danced and drank and enjoyed my hospitality, five thousand warriors traveled through the rift you made in the Waste. They are, as we stand here, waging war on your dear city, and preparing to reclaim what was taken from us. From *me*."

Nausea and horror rush through my body at the thought of Vyrin's forces taking over Night. My home. And following on the heels of that emotion is *rage*. It is not black, it is violet, that heart of wild magic within me.

"You're making a grave error," I say, my voice burning with the flame of that power. "You cannot control the magic of Night."

Vyrin's face twists, his beautiful features morphing. For a moment, I swear I see ram's horns sprouting from his head and fangs protruding from his mouth, superimposed over his own skull.

"I am the creator of you *all*," he intones, and his voice resonates around the room. "I was here at the dawn of time, and I will be here when the earth dissolves into the blood-red sea. I will be the stardust that remains, eons after you are dead and devoured by worms. There is *no* magic I cannot master."

A shiver runs through me, and Asher takes a step closer.

"This is what I will do, to make you pay for your

123

crimes. Crimes of the highest order." Vyrin points at Asher. "I am going to take you with me in three days time, when your city has fallen to its knees and is no longer recognizable. We will travel there so you can stare upon the waste of everything you built, and I will *taste* your pain. Then I will chain you up somewhere with a good view of the destruction and watch as you waste away, deprived of blood and souls, going mad from hunger. And then, I will revive you just before you expire so I can start the whole process again."

Asher trembles with fury beside me and the line that runs between us, the string of wild magic that connects me to him, burns hotter than a star.

"But first," Vyrin says, and his gaze pivots to mine. "*First*, I will spend those three days enjoying your little blood slave in all the ways I know you do. Because we both know she's more than that. And I'm going to find out exactly how much more."

"If you touch me, I will kill you slowly in ways your imagination cannot comprehend," I growl.

Vyrin laughs again. "It would bring me *great* pleasure to see you try."

He makes a gesture, and the guards at our back swarm us.

There are only a dozen of them, and within moments we've taken them all down, even without weapons. That, however, is when the other three dozen, who'd been lined up along the walls, come rushing to their aid. And the tiny glimmer of magic we'd recovered isn't enough to fight off that many.

They drag us apart, leading us in opposite directions.

"Zara!" Asher yells.

I struggle against my captors, but a moment later there's a sharp pain at the back of my head, and darkness sweeps in.

EIGHTEEN

ZARA

I rise from unconsciousness kicking and swinging. But Vyrin is sitting on the other side of the room.

"There's no need for panic, Zara," he says, staring at me in amusement.

Now that Vyrin has made his intentions clear, and any kind of peaceful negotiations are off the table, I don't bite my tongue as I have ever since we stepped foot in this place.

"You've abducted me and made it clear you intend to torture me and my companion while you wage war on our home." My eyes lock onto his. "But I'm not panicking. I just have no intention of sitting back while you implement your plan."

"I can certainly admire that," Vyrin says. "Though, you've misread my intentions. I don't plan to torture you. We're going to have a discussion, after which I feel confident we're going to come to an agreement."

"You're delusional if you think I'd agree to anything after what you just said in the throne room." My fists clench and unclench at my sides.

"Then you're not interested in saving the life of your lord and consort?" Vyrin raises both brows. "Surely you'll at least hear me out. Have a seat." He gestures for a chair not far from his.

I cross my arms over my chest. "I'll stand."

Vyrin shrugs. "You can paint me as the villain in this story if you wish. But you were not alive when it all began. I can taste your... *newness.*"

I fight to suppress the shiver his words send up my spine. How he knows my age, I don't know. And the idea of him tasting anything of mine is repulsive.

"Your so-called Lord of Night and his father struck the first blow, all those centuries ago. They are the ones who shattered the peace between our realms. And they are the ones who stole the magic and walled themselves off from the rest of the world to keep it all to themselves."

"We've already explained that was a terrible tragedy."

"And I've already said I don't believe you." Vyrin taps his fingers on the arm of his chair in agitation. "I am the ruler of all this land, and my blood runs in the veins of all its inhabitants. Even yours, shadow witch. You are fae, same as I. You cannot deny your king."

"Even if that's true, it doesn't mean we're beholden to you," I growl. "You can't torture and kill just because you're the king."

Vyrin's sharp laughter cuts the air. "Why, my darling,

that's *exactly* what it means to be king. I can do whatever I want to whomever I want whenever I want. That's what it means to have *power*."

"But you don't have power, do you?" I'm playing a dangerous game, but I can't stop now that I've started. My words cut as if I still had my daggers. "You said it yourself: you lost your magic. And that magic has become so bottled up it's now tearing our city apart at the seams. There are few who can control it, and you're planning to kill one of them."

"Ahh, but he isn't the only one who can wield the wild magic, is he?" Vyrin's gaze locks on mine, deadly and dark as midnight. "That's what I have *you* for."

"You think I can wield it?" I scoff, trying to throw him off.

"I don't think. I *know*." Vyrin makes a gesture with one hand. "Really, Zara. I told you how ancient I am. How close I am to the magic. You think I can't tell?"

"Then you should know you can't kill Asher. You need both of us if you want to regain control of the magic."

"Just because it took the two of you to wield it doesn't mean that I cannot wield it alone." Vyrin's eyes burn into mine, cruel and predatorial. "I don't need either of you. But you I will keep, until the end of your very long days. You are the ultimate tool of vengeance against the demon king's son. Because he loves you, and you are now *mine*."

CHAPTER
NINETEEN
ASHER

The guards drag me away from Zara. Fury and rage pump through my veins with such intensity it feels like I'll burst into flames at any moment. Several times I break free, adrenaline surging, anger propelling me. I use the tiny glimmer of magic within me, managing to rip the souls from three of the guards, but then the other dozen are upon me.

I don't realize I've been knocked unconscious until I awaken in a prison cell.

I am somewhere far beneath the castle. I can tell that much from the crash of waves against the walls, a sound that comes from *above* me. The air is damp and reeks of mold and decay. I am fairly certain someone is decomposing nearby. In the flickering of torchlight down the hallway outside my cell, I can see the bars of my small enclosure. I am alone.

The reality of the situation pounds against me like the waves against the cliff outside.

It's just as horrifying as I'd imagined it, a nightmare come to life: Zara in the hands of Vyrin. Trapped down here where I can't protect her. The thought of him possessing her in every way makes me insane. He will be as cruel and twisted as possible, all to harm *me*.

I climb to my feet and hurl myself against the bars of my cell over and over again. Even without magic I possess greater than average strength. But the metal holds, even after I batter it for countless minutes. Finally, I sink to the ground, my breathing rapid, my heart pounding. I force myself to slow down and think.

Zara is far from defenseless, even without magic. She's certainly not going to let Vyrin have his way without a terrible fight. But as he'd said, he's ancient. He is clever and powerful, even if his magic is diminished. And his rule here is absolute. The more Zara fights, the more pleasure he'll take from it.

I don't know how I'm going to get out of here, but when I do, I'm going to burn down this entire castle, and Vyrin in it. I will burn field and forest, I will lay such waste to this place that no one will step foot here again. Then I will dig up his burnt bones and give them to a pack of dogs for playthings.

Vyrin may have the upper hand right now, but he made one grave, reckless mistake.

He should have killed me when he had the chance.

CHAPTER
TWENTY
ZARA

I stare at Vyrin, his words echoing in my mind. *Because he loves you, and you are now mine.*

Everyone seems to think they can lay claim to me, possess me, as if I am merely some object to be stolen and placed upon a shelf. Rage simmers in my belly, but I bite back my response. Clearly my attempt to convince him he needs both me and Asher to control Night is a lost cause.

I need to get this conversation turned around.

"You mentioned coming to an agreement," I say. "But all I've heard is threats."

Vyrin's anger morphs into a smug smile. "How quickly you become agreeable, Zara, when you realize you can't win."

It takes every ounce of willpower to suppress a response.

133

"Come, sit by me," he says, pointing to the chair across from him.

Everything within me screams in protest, but I force my feet to move, slowly carrying me across the room. I'll let him think I'm being compliant. Had he any sense at all, he wouldn't wish for me to sit so close to him.

I fold myself into the chair and meet his gaze. "What did you have in mind?"

"I shared my plan with you both earlier," Vyrin begins, leaning back in his chair and fiddling with the tassels on a pillow. "I will annihilate your city, take back my magic, and torture your Lord of Night for hundreds of years. Thousands, perhaps. He will live in agony for an eternity."

The muscles in my cheek begin to twitch and my fingernails dig into the arm of my chair, but I manage to keep my expression neutral.

Vyrin smiles. "However...I could perhaps be more lenient if you and I come to an arrangement."

"Yes?" I ask, because he clearly expects a response. Though it's not hard to imagine what he has in mind.

"You will become my consort. You will give yourself to me in the most intimate ways, and you will accompany me on all my visits to the demon king's son, where we will demonstrate to him the *full* depths of our arrangement." The smile twists even more.

I try not to imagine the horror of what he describes— not only being intimate with this sadist, but doing so in front of Asher. It's a struggle to keep my tone level. "And in exchange?"

"In exchange, I will spare some of the citizens of your city, rather than exterminating them all. And I will allow your former consort every other year in a prison cell being fed a small ration of blood rather than the constant starvation I otherwise have planned for him."

"I see." I make a show of biting my lip, forehead furrowed as if in deep contemplation.

Vyrin raises a brow. "Do you not think it a generous offer?"

I pause just long enough for him to clench his jaw in anger, and then I dip my head. "It is generous."

Another smile. "We are in agreement, then?"

I nod slowly.

He raises a finger and gestures for me. "I require a more enthusiastic response. Come here and show me how generous you think I am. And how very charitable you will be in return."

My heart races as I stand. I cross the short distance between us until I am standing over Vyrin. Then, slowly, I sit down in his lap, straddling his waist. His eyes glow feverishly as I run my fingers into the hair at the back of his head.

"Yes, Zara," he groans. "You belong to *me* now."

I respond by rotating my hands, fast as lightning, and snapping his spinal cord.

His head lulls to the side, eyes rolled back. I step backwards off of him and his body slumps over in its chair.

"You may have been around since the dawn of time, but you still think with your dick." I shake my head.

I know that one such as him can't possibly be killed that easily. But it's bought me enough time to find Asher and get out of this terrible place.

Casting one last glance at the mad fae's limp body, I head for the door.

CHAPTER
TWENTY-ONE
ASHER

The desire for vengeance propels me to my feet and I begin to pace back and forth in front of the bars of my cell. I may have expended the small spark of magic that returned to me, but the fact that it *had* returned means two very important things.

It's not gone forever.

And I can get it back again.

I focus on my rage, remembering that day centuries ago when I summoned the great force that nearly consumed me and Night both. I will get back my power by any means necessary. I have to, to save Zara and my city both. Vyrin will not take them. I won't allow it.

A spark stirs deep in my chest, right at the same moment that footsteps ring from the floor above.

And then Zara steps into view, rushing down the stone steps.

"Dark goddess!" I murmur as she approaches. "How did you—did he—"

"I'm fine," she gasps, breathless, chest heaving.

There's a bloody gash on her right temple, almost blending with her hairline. "What happened?"

"Just a run-in with some guards. I used my magic to get away." She bites her lip. "The last of it, I'm afraid."

"And Vyrin?"

"Incapacitated. For now." Zara places her hands on the bars of the cell. "We need more magic if we're going to make it out of here."

It takes me only a half moment to ascertain her meaning.

"I know you're still angry with me, and that this isn't... *ideal*," she continues. "But if it's the only way to get our magic back..."

She trails off, her eyes burning into mine.

I don't want to admit to Zara—or myself—how much I *need* her right now. Not just to create enough magic for us to escape. But seeing her here, alive, unharmed, when I thought she was being tortured by my greatest enemy... I'm so overwhelmed with relief that I don't care right now about the lies and deceit that hang between us. I don't care about anything but Zara's body in the circle of mine.

A low growl rumbles through my chest. "Turn around."

Zara blinks for a moment, then slowly does as I say. I step up to the bars of the cell and press myself against her from behind. One hand circles around the front of her, crossing over her hip, and the other wraps around the slender column of her throat, holding her head in place. I press my face into her dark hair and inhale deeply. I can hear her heart accelerate at my touch.

My fingers brush her hair behind one ear and I flick my tongue against her earlobe as my other hand moves to the buttons at the front of her pants. Zara shudders against me, a sigh rushing from her lips. My lips and teeth tease down her neck. I get her pants unfastened and yank them down, just enough to expose the V between her legs.

"Asher," Zara gasps. "We need to hurry."

Just the sound of her voice makes me harder than I already am.

"The stronger the release, the stronger the magic," I whisper in her ear. Then I sink my teeth into her neck at the same moment I plunge my finger deep inside her.

Zara cries out as I enter her in two places simultaneously, her knees buckling as she sags against the bars. I hold her tightly in place, both with my hand that's penetrating hard and fast between her legs, and with the other that's around her neck. She's eliciting moans that are driving me wild. Her blood flows into my mouth like liquid gold, like stardust and sunshine mixed.

I pull out my teeth and take my hand from her neck just long enough to unbutton my own pants, not pausing in my onslaught with the other hand. Zara is already so slick, so ready, I can barely see straight. The need to be inside her has reached an animalistic level of desire. When the length of my cock emerges from my pants, I position myself between the bars, pulling Zara even closer, her ass pressing into me. She lets out a small whimper.

I plunge into her from behind, growling as we crash together. Zara shudders again and cries out. My hand that had been inside her moves slightly north, circling over her clit as I thrust into her, and my other hand wraps around her neck again. We're shaking the bars of the cell, the cold metal heating up as our bodies press into it.

Wild magic begins to spark between us, a surge of violet light that wraps from Zara to me and back again. With every thrust it brightens, glowing across the subterranean room and filling me with power. Our cries drown out the crashing of the waves above, and all I know for an unknown span of time is Zara's skin, the heady scent of our sex, and the feel of her pulse against my fingers.

When she starts to shake and cry out, I let myself go along with her. The pleasure and the magic that had been building between us shoots outward, a storm within the stone walls of this place, a violent release born of desperation and longing. I crush Zara against me as we dissolve into each other, as the magic claims us and saves us both. In this moment, I don't ever want to let her go. Not for anything.

But the moment passes, and the light subsides, and reality rushes back in.

Zara calls to her magic, a swell of power I can feel as if it's in my own body, and she bends shadows, pulling me through the bars of the cell.

I know I shouldn't kiss her, because we don't have

time, and I don't know where things stand between us, and it's intimate in a way that the sex was not. But I do kiss her, a tangle of heat and tongues and wishes that can never be fulfilled...pasts that can't be erased and a present that couldn't be more fraught with peril if we tried.

Zara pulls back first. "Are you ready?" she asks.

I palm a ball of magic in my hand, a glowing violet flame. I'm still not back to full power, to the level of strength I had back in Night, but it's a substantial increase from what we generated a few hours before.

"Let's go."

I lead the way as we make our escape.

CHAPTER
TWENTY-TWO

ZARA

W̲e climb the stone steps from the lowest level of the dungeon cells. This is the second time I've escaped a prison in the last two days. I hope it will be the last.

There aren't any other prisoners down here. I'm not sure if that means there's another prison block somewhere, or if it means that Vyrin doesn't usually take prisoners at all. There had only been two guards at the main entrance three floors above, guards I'd disabled on my way down. But when we reach the door leading out into the castle, they aren't there.

"The guards must have woken up," I say, pointing to the corner where I'd dragged their bodies a few minutes before.

"Then they'll have gone for reinforcements," Asher says. "Let's get out of here before they're back."

He looks left and right down the hall, seeming unsure

which way to go, so I take the lead. I'd found my way down here following the connection of magic that runs between us, and I'd made sure to note my path for the journey back. Though I don't want to head back toward Vyrin's quarters.

When we reach the juncture in our path that leads toward that part of the castle, I turn the opposite direction. "I'm not sure the quickest way from here," I admit.

Voices ring out in the hall behind us, and we plunge ahead. I call on my shadows, feeling a rush of warmth, a feeling like coming home. It feels so amazing to have my magic back, even if it's just a fraction of what it used to be. We actually have a fighting chance now.

Guards burst through a door a few yards ahead of us, and I have no choice but to dart into a hall on the right. Is Vyrin recovered, or did someone just find his body and raise the alarm? I wish with everything inside of me that he's good and truly dead, but I know it can't be that easy. Not someone as old as he claims to be, the maker of all fae.

We run into a wide hallway that I recognize from the day before, and Asher and I look at each other and nod. He clearly recognizes it, too. A left turn leads us toward the front gates of the castle. Which, of course, is guarded by two dozen warriors. But now we have magic, and the taste of freedom, and hell on our heels.

Screams ring out as we approach the gate and the warriors flank out to block our path, weapons drawn. Behind us comes a chorus of yells as well, echoing down the stone halls. I call on my magic and my shadows and I wrap them around me and Asher both. We vanish from sight as we charge the front gate.

Confusion and panic bloom on the faces of the guards as we approach. Asher begins to rip souls from bodies as we move closer. The first body falls like a puppet with its strings cut, falling limp to the ground, along with a swell of energy as the life force of the guard moves into Asher's body. Another falls, then another, then another. Asher bellows as he absorbs their energy, and the faces of the remaining warriors contort in fear.

When we're a dozen feet away, I send a surge of magic outward, a blast like storm winds. It knocks the remaining guards to their feet and we fly past them. I hit the lever managing the portcullis with another blast of magic, and the gate groans and slowly begins to rise. We don't wait for it to get all the way to its apex. Diving underneath, we roll to freedom and then send a blast of magic into the gate mechanism, sending the thing crashing down behind us to block our pursuers. The lever shatters, wood flying everywhere.

It's not over yet, though.

From the direction of the rift, a battalion of cavalry on those massive bronze horses comes galloping over the hill. They must have heard the destruction of the portcullis or seen us break out of the entrance. Whatever the case, we're now facing two dozen mounted horsemen, and they're blocking the path between us and the way back home.

"The Thorn Forest!" Asher cries, grabbing my arm and turning me around. "It's our best chance."

I nod and we run for the dark, looming tree line ahead. It's a good half-mile off, and with the speed of the beasts running up behind us, we're not going to make it. I call on magic again to make me run faster, and Asher does the same. The land blurs by, green and gold as the sun climbs the sky.

Magic buzzes through my veins but I can feel the finiteness of it, can feel it draining out of me. Back in Night I had to worry about the opposite—letting in so much magic that it burned me up, me and everything around me. How the tables have turned. I would give anything to feel that swell of endless power now, that all-consuming force within me.

There's only a bit left, our mad fight for freedom having drained most of it. We're almost to the trees now, the twisted, thorn-covered trunks clawing at the pale blue sky. Hoofbeats pound so loudly behind us they shake the earth. We're so close... if we got this far only to fail now...

Asher and I plunge into the forest, darting between the trunks and branches and thick, thorny vines. The horses scream as they pull up short behind us, forced to slow so the riders can dismount. Darkness falls around us, so thick are the branches overhead. I can barely see the sun at all, as if dawn gave up and relinquished back into night. The howl of a dog cuts through the air, and then another. A whole pack of them.

They're hunting us.

Sounds of pursuit punctuate the sharp gasp of my lungs, the beating of my heart. My feet strangely make almost no sound at all in the mossy, loamy soil. I can feel the last of my magic drain out of me. I'm not sure how much longer we can make it with dozens of warriors at our backs, and no magic to fight with. An arrow whistles past my head, then another.

And then, one of the trees directly in front of us, a gnarled, massive thing with a trunk as big around as a castle tower, opens. A yawning door leading into darkness.

A lone figure stands in the opening of the tree.

TWENTY-THREE

For a moment I think the woman standing in the tree is a specter of some sort, a spirit of the forest, so quickly does she appear. But she looks quite solid, and she also looks quite familiar.

As if she could be Zara's twin.

Zara stops dead in her tracks like she's been slapped in the face.

"Follow me if you want to live," her sister says, beckoning and disappearing within the tree just as quickly as she'd appeared.

The voices of our pursuers and the howls of their dogs are far too close for me to consider it twice. I shove Zara, who seems frozen in shock, forward into the tree, and then I follow. A moment later I hear a scratching, scraping sound and a crunch as the door in the tree closes behind us.

We're plunged into darkness for a moment before a light flares to life a couple feet away. Zara's sister is standing over what appears to be a hole leading down into the earth. She carries a small stone which emits a soft glow. It illuminates the inside of the hollowed-out tree trunk, which is large enough for five men to stand shoulder-to-shoulder. I can see now that the door in the tree is made with a clever system of ropes and levers. It's all a bit mind boggling.

But most of all—how in the name of the dark goddess did Zara's sister get here?

We must both be staring at her, because she makes an impatient sound. "Now! Before the dogs circle back and realize where you went."

She disappears into the hole without further discussion. Zara, face still stricken, follows her. I take up the rear, and I realize as I follow that there's an extremely narrow set of earthen steps built into the earth, spiraling down and away from the hollow tree. Within a dozen steps we're beneath the tree, its roots dangling from the earthen ceiling over our heads. A dark, narrow tunnel leads away from the base of the stairs.

Jaylen strides down the tunnel without a backward glance. It's surreal to be rescued and now traversing an underground tunnel with the person we'd come to realize, right before the explosion that took our magic, is Falling Star, the mysterious and faceless leader of the Factionless. Now we know her identity, and she is far from faceless… I can't get over how much she resembles Zara.

The tunnel goes on for quite a ways, a quarter mile at least, before opening onto a much wider tunnel that runs perpendicular in either direction. There's a foul smell on the air here, a bitter smell like burnt flesh. The light from the glowing stone reveals deep gouges in the walls of the new tunnel, gouges that look like…

"Are those claw marks?" Zara whispers, eyes wide.

"Yes," Jaylen says. "Which is why we need to keep moving."

But Zara crosses her arms over her chest, lips set in a stubborn line. "How is it that you're here?"

"I'll explain everything later. Right now, we need to get someplace safe."

Jaylen turns left down the wider tunnel, which seems contrary to her warning from a moment ago, but within a dozen feet she turns right into another smaller tunnel like the one we started on. We travel another good distance, a mile maybe, in dark and silence. Then, Jaylen abruptly begins climbing a wooden ladder that rises through the ceiling of the tunnel and disappears. Zara and I follow yet again.

When my head breaks the surface of the earth about twenty feet above the tunnel floor, I look around to see that we're in a small glen. It's encircled entirely by snarls of vines thick as serpents, with thorns as big as my head. There doesn't appear to be any way in or out other than the tunnel beneath us.

"We can rest here," Jaylen says, gesturing around her.

She sits down a few feet away in the soft moss and takes a swig from the flask at her hip before passing it to Zara. Zara tosses it back, clearly expecting it to be water, but the grimace on her face tells me otherwise. With visible effort, she swallows the liquid, running the back of her hand across her mouth before passing it to me.

"That's Siduri's homemade liquor," Zara says, her tone accusatory, her eyes burning into Jaylen's.

I sit down next to Zara and take my own sip, a much smaller one. The liquid burns as it goes down my throat but creates a lovely warmth in my chest to balance the pain. I have no idea who Siduri is, but she makes good alcohol.

"It is," Jaylen responds. "But since you're no doubt wondering, no, she doesn't know who I am."

"I appreciate the help back there," Zara says, taking the flask from me and passing it back to her sister. "But I'd really like to know what's going on."

"You're not the only one," Jaylen says. Her eyes narrow and look past Zara to me. "I'd like to know how my sister fell in with the destroyer of Night."

I tense, but Zara shoots me a look that tells me to keep quiet. There isn't anyone else alive I would heed, except for her. The realization sends a strange prickling sensation through my chest.

"Why don't we start with present day, and then go back to the beginning," Zara suggests.

Jaylen nods. She's silent for a long moment, and then she begins.

TWENTY-FOUR

ZARA

I stare into the purple eyes of my sister, eyes that are so very similar to mine. To our mother's.

"How I got here is simple enough," Jaylen says. "After the magical explosion in Night, I escaped before the Angelus and Animus warriors arrived." Her eyes grow distant for a moment. "To be honest, I wasn't sure you deserved saving, not after seeing you with *him*."

Jaylen's eyes fixate on Asher, burning with hatred. I shoot him another look of warning.

"But when my network of spies caught wind that you were being sent through the rift to Vyrin, I couldn't just let you go. I followed you to Vyrin's castle. Well, outside of his castle - I knew better than to go inside. I waited, and I hoped you'd come back out. And I was ready when you did."

I turn this over in my mind, shaking my head. "The

rumors of Falling Star… they said you could travel through the Waste. But how?"

Jaylen merely shakes her head. "Later. It's your turn now. How did you fall in with him?" She jerks her head toward Asher.

I take a deep breath, my eyes darting a half-moment to Asher. "After escaping the prison camp, I was captured by House Animus. I've lived among them the last decade. And then, recently, I was sent to spy on the Lord of Night, to gain his trust, so that eventually I could kill him."

At this Jaylen's eyes widen, and she looks back and forth from me to Asher, clearly trying to judge his reaction. My stomach twists, a knot forming. I don't want to recount the story that drove a wedge between us. A thorn bigger than the ones surrounding us now.

"But I learned that many of the things I was told about the Lord of Night were wrong. Were lies. And I grew to trust him more than the man who tutored me. We realized that we shared a connection to the wild magic, a connection that might help us save our goddess-forsaken city." I draw in a shuddering breath. "Except then a crazy angel detonated a magical device that ruined everything and plunged us even further into chaos than we were before."

Jaylen's expression had grown more skeptical with each word that left my mouth. "So, you expect me to believe that this man can save our city, just because you fell in love with him?"

Asher's chin jerks toward mine, but I keep my gaze firmly on Jaylen. "Your turn," I say softly.

Jaylen crosses her arms over her chest but nods in acquiescence. "Fine. You want to know how I'm able to cross the Waste? I suppose for that, we have to go back to the beginning. To the day I was taken from the prison camp."

My breath catches in my chest. That day had changed the entire trajectory of my life.

"I was supposed to go to the Palace of Night." Jaylen's eyes flick to Asher. "But Factionless intercepted the caravan, and several of us were taken."

I nod. I'd discovered that much myself just recently.

"The Factionless who rescued me were part of a group obsessed with finding a way across the Waste. For years they failed at their attempts, always ending in someone's horrific death. I should have been scared after hearing so many tales. But over the years, I realized that Night was no better. Every day people were dying from the war, or from a surge in the wild magic."

Jaylen pauses and draws in a shaky breath.

"I realized that Death walked at my shoulder no matter what direction I traveled. So, I decided if I was going to die, it would be in a manner of my choosing. Not at the mercy of things I couldn't control inside the boundaries of Night. So," she says. "I set out across the Waste alone. And that was the day I found the monsters everyone talked about. Or rather, the wyrm found me."

"Wyrm?" Asher asks, brow wrinkled.

"The thing that made those tunnels."

"But you survived," I say in awe.

Jaylen smiles and takes a swig from her flask. "Your turn."

I nod. "So…you don't believe Asher can save Night. I don't blame you. I hated him half my life. And I would still hate him if it weren't for Night herself… for the magic that runs through her veins. But we share a connection through that magic. So yes, especially now, since Vyrin has apparently sent an army through the rift to destroy our city, I believe that Asher and I are the only ones who can save Night."

"You speak of Night as if she's a living thing." Jaylen's expression is blank. It's a statement more than a question.

"She is," I respond simply. "I can feel her presence."

Jaylen appraises me for several long moments. Then she says, "My turn, I suppose." She pauses, seeming to collect her thoughts, or perhaps just remembering. "The day I tried to cross the Waste, the wyrm—the great earth serpent—burst up out of the earth. But it missed me by a hair, and so instead of falling into its jaws, I fell alongside its body, down into the tunnel it had created. I escaped through those tunnels. And eventually I mapped them all out and crossed into Cyrena. Learned of Vyrin and the people there. Traveled unknown and unseen between the two lands. Met a few friends along the way that I shared my secret with. And the rest you know."

"The rest I do *not* know," I say. "Why did you assume the identity of Falling Star if you cared so little for Night? Why come back at all?"

Jaylen's face sours. "No doubt you think I should have abandoned hope, given up. As you abandoned me."

My body goes rigid. "Abandoned you?! I have spent my entire life since the day you were taken thinking of nothing *but* you. Trying to avenge your death!"

"My death?" Jaylen snarls.

"The Animus captured me when I was trying to break into the Palace of Night to save you. The Lord of Animus later told me you were dead." My heart pounds so hard it's painful, my blood rushing too fast. "He lied so he could use me as a pawn, make me more motivated to kill Asher. I have spent the last decade grieving you, planning vengeance for you. Everything I have done I have done for *you*."

Jaylen falls silent, then gets up and strides across the glen. I look over at Asher, who gives me a nod of encouragement, and I follow her. When I reach her she's facing away from me, standing nearly up against one of the thorn trees.

As I step up behind her, Jaylen speaks, so quietly it's barely a whisper. "This whole time, I thought you were a coward, that you hid and let them take me. I *hated* you for it."

Sorrow washes through me, icy and sharp as knives. "I'm sorry you thought I abandoned you. I would never abandon my little sister."

She turns, slowly. "But I abandoned *you*. I never came looking for you. I was so angry. I've wasted so much time…"

157

"How would you have found me, even if you tried?" I suck in a shaky breath. "This war, this life… it's nearly impossible. We all do the best we can to survive."

"And you think the Lord of Night can end the war?"

I don't answer for a moment. "I'm not sure anyone can, now that Vyrin has come through the Waste. But we're going to try. Or take our last breaths in the attempt."

"Well then," Jaylen says. "I suppose I'd better show you the way through the tunnels so we can try to save Night before that bastard fae destroys it all."

"We?" I ask, a small smile on my face.

Jaylen nods. "We."

TWENTY-FIVE

When Zara and her sister return from across the glen, there's a lightness between them that wasn't there before. Zara is smiling, something she so rarely does, and I find myself wishing with a fierce and fiery longing for the type of life that would draw out that smile on a daily basis. A life without war and death lingering at each dawn and each moonrise.

I shake my head. Even if we had such a life, I can't have it with Zara. How could I possibly live at peace knowing she spent a decade of her life with my brother? Mentored by him, loved by him?

But I also don't think I can live at peace without her.

"Jaylen is going to help us get back to Night," Zara says.

I look up at them, meeting Jaylen's eyes. "Thank you."

"You can thank Zara," Jaylen gestures to her sister.

"She convinced me that you're worthy of a chance. And we have a city to save, which will take all of us."

I get to my feet. "That it will."

"Before we go, I need to restock on supplies. We'll need food and you two need weapons. Plus, I need to warn my companions on this side of the Waste that Vyrin is invading Night. If he regains his magic…" She trails off a moment. "Things will be dire indeed."

Impatience chafes under my skin. Every minute we spend here is another minute that Night comes closer to destruction. But I'm not going to argue the point when she's agreed to help us. And she's not wrong about food and weapons.

Zara nods, though her lips are set in a grim line as if she's thinking the same thing. "Lead the way."

Jaylen doesn't take us back to the tunnel in the ground. She leads us between two of the huge thorn trees and moves aside a piece of woven vines that I see now is a gate of sorts, cleverly set in place amongst the other branches and vines. After we pass through, she puts it back in place, and it looks as impenetrable as it did before.

The forest is shadowy and hushed as we traverse the mossy ground beneath the twisted black trunks. Here and there we have to duck beneath a gnarled branch or a huge vine covered in deadly thorns. In places the trees are clustered so close together that moving between them brings my face within an inch of a razor-sharp protrusion. I wouldn't be surprised if they were poisonous as well.

While we've got to be at least two miles from where

we entered the forest, I'm relieved not to hear hunting dogs in the distance. Vyrin's guards have either called them off or they've traveled far enough in the wrong direction that they're out of range. Nonetheless, my ears and the rest of my body are on alert. Zara seems tense and at-the-ready as well.

After traveling an hour or more south, which I can tell by the moss growing on the tree trunks, Jaylen halts and turns to face us. We're in an area of the forest where boulders rise from the forest floor and the trees are a bit further apart. I can hear the murmur of a creek in the distance.

"My companions live not far from here. I should go first and explain who you are…they aren't overly fond of outsiders." She pauses, then adds, "There aren't many monsters here in the forest. You should be safe until I get back."

Not *many* monsters. I cross my arms over my chest and let out a snort of mirth, causing Zara to look over at me in surprise.

"We'll be fine," I say.

Jaylen nods and vanishes into the trees ahead.

"What was that about?" Zara asks.

"Well, within Night there are surges of wild magic and warring factions. Here in Cyrena there are evil fae and monsters." I shrug. "I suppose everywhere you go there's something awful to contend with."

Zara contemplates this a moment. "I'm not sure I'd know what to do with myself if there wasn't."

I walk over and lean back against one of the boulders.

"I used to wonder, in my darkest hours, if Night was worth saving. I clung to the idea of unity, of peace, but most of the time I never believed it possible."

Zara watches me with those purple eyes, waiting for me to continue.

"But now that Vyrin is intent on grinding my city beneath his boot, of taking all the magic I struggled to contain these last centuries, I realize how truly bad things can get. How much darker the future could be." I let out a slow breath. "Funny how things can change your perspective in an instant."

Her voice is soft when she answers. "It certainly is."

I realize by her tone, the hollow ring to it, that she means *us*.

My feet lead me to where she stands, without conscious effort to do so. Her arms are crossed over her chest, and she doesn't look at me when I approach. "I wish I could change how I feel about things between us," I say. "But it's not that easy."

Zara finally looks up at me, her eyes full of sorrow. "Nothing ever is."

"You think I can just forget that you were raised and mentored by my brother, who is one of my greatest enemies?"

Her face shifts from sadness to cold anger in the span of a heartbeat. "What I know is that I'm tired of apologizing for my past, a past I had no control over and can't change. If you want to hate me, then hate me."

And she turns and strides away from me into the trees.

TWENTY-SIX

ZARA

I haven't made it ten steps before I hear footsteps behind me. Asher grabs my shoulder and spins me around.

"Don't you dare accuse me of hating you," he growls. "You know that's not true."

"Do I?" I snap. "You told me you never wanted to see me again. You treated me like your blood bag. Now we have a fragile truce only because we need each other to get our magic back. But at every turn, you remind me of how impossible it is that we could ever mend things between us."

"I was angry, but I never hated you," Asher groans. "I want to hate you. *Dark goddess*, it would make things easier."

He reaches up and runs his right hand into my hair, cupping my cheek as he does. His eyes lock onto mine.

"Because if I hated you, I could walk away. But

instead, I have this constant torment inside of me, knowing you used to belong to Kieran, and knowing also that I want you to be mine forever."

I suck in a sharp breath. *Forever...* "Forever is a long time to be in constant torment," I say softly.

"It is," he says, and he kisses me.

And I know the meaning of that same torment, because I want to be angry, to shove him away from me, but at the same time I want his heat and his breath and his skin against mine too badly. Asher kisses me soft and slow, not the desperate crush of lips in the dungeon. He kisses me until the forest turns to stars and everything spins. When my back brushes up against one of the boulders, I let out a gasp of surprise. I hadn't even realized we were moving.

The need to have him inside me is overwhelming. It's not just the desire to feel magic again. He's like an elixir I can't ever get enough of. Even when I'm furious with him, like right now, I *crave* him in a way I don't crave anything else. I know it's not going to change anything between us, but I can't stop myself from wanting him. This burning desire from almost the instant we met, a duality of fury and passion...being able to let myself go completely, something I could never do with anyone else.

I work at the buckle of his pants, tugging it open as he peels mine down, off and over my boots, tossing them to the forest floor. Our eyes meet and lock as Asher slowly slides his enormous length into me. A low moan rises from my throat as pleasure ripples through my core and my eyelids flutter.

I wrap my legs around his hips and my arms around his neck. Asher thrusts again, one arm against the boulder, one wrapped around my back, crushing me into him. When my lashes flutter again and I close my eyes, Asher takes my chin.

"Look at me, Zara," he says. "I want you to look at me when you come."

The sound of his voice, deep as the roots of the earth, makes another shiver of pleasure spike through my body. I lock my gaze back onto his, and I rock my hips forward as he drives into me again. He lets out a low growl. His hips gyrate again, and this time we both moan, magic flaring between us, a spiral of violet light.

Asher picks up the pace just a little, his eyes still on mine as he slides in and out, pushing me up and down the smooth stone. Ecstasy is rippling outward from my core with every thrust, and as it does, our magic grows. I let out a sound that's half-animal as my climax begins to break all around me.

"Wait for me, Zara," Asher commands.

But instead of waiting, I lean down to run my lips along Asher's neck. And then, some wild instinct driving me, I bite him. Hard. As if I'm the one who drinks blood. I bite him so hard that I can taste his blood in my mouth, warm and metallic.

Asher roars and convulses, exploding inside me. The strength of his final thrust sends me over the edge with him, and I cry out as magic and pleasure unfurl within my body. I release his neck and lock my eyes on his, those molten bronze eyes. It feels as if we're melting into each other, like I can feel Asher's bliss along with my own. I don't know where I end and where he begins, the boundaries of my physical body and my magic.

Before my climax subsides, Asher lifts me off the boulder, laying me down in the soft moss on the forest floor. With another growl, he buries his face between my legs. A scream rips from my mouth as another wave of ecstasy consumes me. He is not slow and intimate like he was a moment ago. He is relentless and ravenous like a hungry wolf.

"*Asher*," I moan as he grazes my thigh with his teeth.

He bites into the soft skin of my thigh right next to my sweet core. My hips buck and my back arches up as pleasure spikes through my body. Asher alternates between sucking my bite mark and licking my clit, and within moments I'm shaking as another storm builds inside of me. Magic sparks off my body like a bonfire.

When he's had his fill of blood, he buries his face inside me again, and then I am lost.

I lay there, shaking, for several long moments. I'm pumping with so much magic that my head feels fuzzy. Asher crawls on his hands and knees to lay beside me, kissing my shoulder and the side of my neck, and finally a soft brush over my lips.

"This is the problem, Zara," he murmurs against my skin. "You *are* my torment, but I can't stay away from you. You are my weakness, my undoing."

I go still against him. "I don't want to make you weak."

"It's not your fault…it's our fate, I suppose."

"I know it's not my fault." I push up on one elbow. "You should be angry I was plotting your murder, but instead, you're angry about my past, about things I can't undo."

Asher lies on the forest floor, his eyes closed, for what seems an eternity.

"Right now, we need each other," he finally says, sitting up. He summons a pulse of magic that glows along his skin. "For this."

His gaze moves to mine, then drops again. "But maybe, when we get back to Night and we figure every-thing out—*if* we figure everything out—maybe a bit of distance is what we need. Maybe this terrible torment will lessen over time if we're not constantly…" he waves up and down at our naked bodies.

My throat feels tight. It takes me a moment to find words. "Is-is that what you want? To part ways after the battle is over?"

"No…and yes." Asher shakes his head. "I think we need to at least try."

I stand slowly, extricating myself from the tangle of his limbs. This is worse than when Asher was furious with me, when he was cold and distant. Because I know part of him wants to be with me, but he's not willing to let go of the past. Not more than he wants a future with me.

I had known these precious minutes in the forest

wouldn't change anything, and yet his words still send cracks through my heart. He'd said I was his weakness, but he's mine, too. And I've never let anything make me weak before. Not in my whole life.

He's right. Love is a liability we can't afford.

I find my pants and tug them back on, then I turn to face him. "Agreed. We'll continue our temporary truce to regain our magic, and if we survive the battle against Vyrin, we'll go our separate ways."

TWENTY-SEVEN
ZARA

When we walk back the way we came, Jaylen is there waiting for us. Her eyes widen when she sees me, and she throws her hands in the air.

"I thought you two had been eaten by something! After telling you there weren't monsters in this area..." Her face morphs from surprise to anger. "Don't do that again!"

"Sorry," I say softly.

Jaylen narrows her eyes, cocking her head to the side. "You two are... practically *glowing* with magic all of the sudden."

I duck my head, a blush heating my cheeks, and Jaylen's mouth falls open.

"Oh..."

"After the explosion—we—we lost our magic," I explain haltingly. "But since we share a bond with it... when we're together..."

"I see." Jaylen rocks back on the heels of her boots. "Well, that's about enough sister bonding considering we just reunited. Why don't I introduce you to my companions and you can get some food and weapons."

I nod, relieved at the change of subject. The last thing I want to talk about right now is me and Asher.

"Oh, and when we get there—" Jaylen turns so quickly I almost run into her— "Do not tell them who you are." She directs her comment to Asher, her eyes pinned to his.

His jaw flexes, but he nods. "I take it the Lord of Night is not well regarded in these parts?"

"Most of the people here are refugees from Night. But a handful were born here, in Cyrena. They have no magic, and Vyrin has told everyone for decades that you stole their magic." Jaylen's lips are set in a firm line. "Even I can't protect you if they discover who you are."

We continue walking, but Jaylen's words pique my curiosity.

"So, those born in Night possess magic, but those born here do not..." I muse aloud. "Doesn't that cause strife among you?"

Jaylen shrugs. "When we explain the situation in Night, most do not wish to wield magic so badly as to live in a war-torn city, subjected to potential death anytime you cast a spell. Or even if you don't, and there's a random surge." She looks over at me. "Besides, the longer one of us is gone from Night, the weaker our magic becomes, until eventually, it vanishes altogether."

Asher raises his brows. "Really?"

Jaylen nods. "Our camp is almost entirely Incantrix, with a couple Animus. The Animus can still shift at the full moon, but they cannot wield any other magic."

"But when you travel back to Night, your magic is replenished?" I ask.

"Yes." She confirms. "The moment I step foot in the city it comes rushing back to me."

Asher shakes his head, his expression stormy. "I never imagined...never knew the damage I caused to the rest of Aureon."

We fall silent, and Jaylen leads the way through the forest, about a quarter mile to a huge, twisted tree. It's easily three times as large as the rest, not just in height but in girth. It would take twenty men to circle the thing, arms stretched. Mist curls around the trunk of the thing like silver snakes along the forest floor.

Like the tree Jaylen first appeared in, this one has a hidden door which she activates by pressing a series of knobs cleverly concealed in the bark. A small gap appears and she ducks through, gesturing for us to follow. When I step into the shadowy interior of the tree, I'm greeted by two armed guards, one on each side of the hollowed-out trunk. They're wearing simple garb: brown pants, boots, and tunics which I imagine help them blend into the forest.

They cast wary glances at me and Asher, their eyes following us as we pass by them, though they don't move a muscle. Long bows are strapped to their backs, and they carry several daggers each. Blocks of ice would have provided a warmer welcome than these two. Jaylen was right when she said they don't like outsiders.

I hear the sound of wood creaking as the door closes behind us again, and we're plunged into total darkness for a moment. Then Jaylen presses something on the other side of the trunk and another door opens. The dim ocher light of the forest reveals an entirely unexpected landscape.

We're standing at the edge of a narrow ravine that splits the forest floor. Steep, earthen steps banked by fallen logs lead down to the bottom of it. It runs as far as I can see before twisting sharply and disappearing from view. The sides of the ravine are so steep that one would have to rappel into the interior to access it from above, which would be seriously hindered by the barricade of thorny vines hanging near the apex.

I follow Jaylen down the steps, Asher at my back. The smell of woodfire and cooking meat hits my nose, and I realize how starved I am. It's been at least a day since I've eaten, what with not being able to consume any of the fae food. As we reach the floor of the ravine, I see a couple dozen people at least. Sitting around fires, sharpening weapons, flocking arrows, stirring soup. Several call greetings to Jaylen, but Asher and I receive the same frigid stares the guards above had given us.

It hits me, then. My sister has a family here. And she has a life in Night as well. A whole life that I've missed for the last ten years. The last time I saw her, she was a child. Now she is grown, and she is fierce and brave and has survived against all odds, through war and the Waste both. There's been a void inside me this whole time, a missing piece where she belonged, but now it feels even bigger knowing that all of this transpired, all this time we could have had together. It feels as if I've been gutted, a pain as sharp as a blade.

"Are you okay?" Asher asks softly, looking down at me, brow furrowed.

I hadn't even noticed him at my shoulder. His concern just twists the knife even deeper. I don't want his concern or his pity. He's made it clear there is nothing between us. So, I just nod my head, a sharp jerk of the chin, and keep walking.

Jaylen stops in front of a small wooden hut made from branches and vines woven together. An old man sits in a woven chair beneath a small overhang that serves as a porch. He is about as gnarled as the thorn trees, with skin to match. Tufts of white hair poke out beneath a small brown cap over his head. His ears are slightly pointed at the tips.

"Elden, greetings." Jaylen inclines her head. "These are the friends I mentioned. They are in need of weapons to cross the Waste."

The old man, Elden, stares up at me for a moment, then turns his gaze to Asher. His eyes are a startling green as bright as the moss along the forest floor. "Aye," he grunts.

"Though they seem to possess a fair amount of magic that will be of better use to them than any blade."

"The magic is unpredictable of late," Jaylen says. "Best to have a back-up."

Elden grunts again and rises slowly from his chair. "That be true." He shoots me a suspicious look, and Asher, too. "Wait here. Let me see what I'm willing to part with. It won't come cheap."

Jaylen rolls her eyes. "You know I'm good for it."

The old man grumbles and shuffles into his hut.

"I'm going to step over there and get you some food," Jaylen says. "Be right back."

I watch her as she walks to a small fire around which three people sit. They shoot us glances as Jaylen approaches, but they don't seem quite as begrudging about offering assistance as old Elden. A man gets out of his seat and helps Jaylen ladle soup into two small wooden bowls, placing a large hunk of bread into each one.

When she returns and passes a bowl to each of us, Asher starts to shake his head, but Jaylen makes a low sound in her throat and shoots him a pointed look. Apparently the Daemonium are not well-regarded here. He takes the bowl without another word and we follow Jaylen to a bench made of logs not far from the fire. We both begin to eat, me far more hungrily than him, since he's had plenty of my blood.

As we eat, one of the men by the fire starts to play music on a small hand pipe. The notes rise into the air along with the smoke, sweet and melancholy both. I can't remember the last time I heard music, or saw people just sitting around relaxing. Not gearing up for battle or huddling in dark alleyways or calling on magic that might kill them.

I eat my food too quickly, my stomach still growling. Without saying a word, Asher places his piece of bread into my bowl. His kindness makes me want to slap him. I want to be angry with him so badly. But I'm too hungry to be stubborn about it, so I devour the second piece of bread, feeling much better for having had it.

Meanwhile, the pipe player has changed beats to a melody with a fast tempo. Two of the women get up and hook their arms together and begin laughing and dancing around the fire. A couple other people join, and one drags Jaylen out to join them. I expect her to protest, my sister who is the secret leader of the rebels of Night, renowned and worshipped like a goddess. But she just grins and allows herself to be swept along into the merriment.

A strange sensation moves through my chest as I watch them. A feeling of joy mingled with deep, deep sorrow. My whole body goes rigid as I watch. I have never witnessed this kind of carefree behavior, and so I never even imagined it could exist. I have known nothing but the constant danger and darkness in my city.

Night holds my heart and my soul. All of it. Or so I thought, until this very moment. Because watching these people makes me realize I know nothing of this world.

Nothing but my tiny, tiny corner of it. I realize with deep certainty, as I watch them, that I want to see what else lies beyond the walls of my prison. How far does Aureon stretch? What other kinds of people and beasts wander it?

And most importantly, who am I when I am not trapped within the boundaries I have always known?

"You don't like the music?" Asher asks softly, startling me from my thoughts.

My brows shoot up. "What makes you say that?"

"Because you were frowning."

I shrug. "Just thinking."

"Anything I should worry about?"

He shoots me a look of concern, and once again I feel those tiny cracks working through my heart.

"Nothing you need to concern yourself with," I say, standing.

I leave my bowl on the log and turn to go check on the old man who's gathering our supplies. Inside the hut, I can hear clanging and banging as Elden sorts through weapons. I don't intend on trying to rush the man, but I also don't want to sit with Asher any longer.

A couple minutes later, he finally emerges with three small steel daggers, a large battle axe, and several small, fat brown sticks. I eye the latter with an apparent question on my face, because Jaylen walks up behind me and says, "Flares. In case we need a distraction."

"You light them with flame or magic," Elden adds, pointing to small strings at the ends of each one.

I don't want to think about the kind of creatures we'll

need to distract with flares. Just the memory of the thing that attacked us on the way across the Waste makes me shiver. But I remind myself that my sister has made this voyage many times.

"Thank you, Elden," I say, and Asher, who has joined us, adds his thanks as well.

Asher takes the axe and one of the daggers, and I take the other two, strapping one to my belt holster and the other inside my boot. We each take a flare, and Jaylen takes a third.

"Well, let's be on our way, then," she says.

She waves goodbye to her companions and we make our way back down the ravine the way we'd come, heading for the earthen stairs and the enormous tree. I take it all in as we move. I've never seen anything like this place. I can still hear the music, and my thoughts return again to what other wonders lie beyond this forest. For one wild moment I imagine what it might be like to turn in the opposite direction, to leave Night and never return. But my heart lies there, even as broken as it is. I can't give up on it, even though it will likely claim my life.

As we approach the steps leading out of the ravine, I hear a clamoring of voices, as if some sort of argument has broken out. Jaylen looks over her shoulder and her expression grows grim. She gestures for us to move up the stairs ahead of her.

But as Asher climbs the first step, a voice booms out across the ravine.

"I know you!"

I turn now, too, and above me, Asher places his hand on the axe at his side. A tall mountain of a man lumbers toward us, murder in his eyes. He raises a massive arm and jabs it toward Asher.

"Lord of Night!" the man bellows. "You killed my father. You owe me a blood debt."

TWENTY-EIGHT

ASHER

I stare at the man before me, his face twisted in rage. There's no point asking who his father is. I have killed so many in my long life. Was it in battle, or a flare of wild magic? Or did I claim his soul to keep my hunger at bay, the unending hunger that is my dark curse?

It doesn't matter, in the end. The result is the same.

"I'm sorry if I have taken someone you loved," I call, my voice ringing across the gathering crowd.

"Your apology means nothing to me, demon." The man rears his head back and spits on the ground.

"We are on a mission of utmost importance," Jaylen calls. "I must ask that you let us pass peacefully."

"Did you know who this man is, Jaylen?" The huge man snarls, stabbing a finger in my direction. "And you brought him here, into our home?"

A couple feet away from me, both Jaylen and Zara go rigid. I can't endanger Zara's sister, not after she saved us.

And because I know that Zara will never, ever forgive me. After all, it's the entire reason she plotted my death for years.

"I will pay your blood debt!" I shout, making sure all can hear. "Is it combat that you wish?"

"I want your head on a spike," the man growls.

"Very well," I say. "If you can take it from my shoulders, it's yours."

Zara turns her head slowly and stares up at me, her expression inscrutable. She's said almost nothing to me since we joined together in the forest. If I die here, that conversation will be the last we ever had.

It makes me sick to think of it. But there's nothing to be done for it now.

"Does everyone here bear witness to this blood challenge?" My accuser bellows.

A chorus of *ayes* rise throughout the ravine. They all seem just as eager to spill my blood as he is. I could sense it from the moment we'd stepped foot in this place.

"There are no rules in this combat," he continues. "Other than the challenge ends when one of the combatants is dead."

A small ripple of magic moves off of Zara, but I rest my hand on her shoulder and squeeze.

"I do not wish to kill you," I call to my challenger. "Are you sure first blood is not what you seek?"

"You will not kill me." The man smiles. "Because you will not be fighting me. You will be fighting my *beast*."

A round of cheers moves across the crowd, and Jaylen

turns and shoots me a look that tells me my life is forfeit. I'd figured the man wouldn't be satisfied with first blood, but I had to offer, since taking the life of both him and his father seems unnecessarily cruel. It seems, however, that he had other plans all along.

It's too late to back out now, and I owe this man a blood debt either way. I nod. "Let's proceed, then."

The crowd swarms around me, Zara, and Jaylen, sweeping us back down the ravine as if we're going to try to escape. Chanting arises, with calls of "Jodin! Jodin!" which I can only guess is the name of the man who challenged me. There are also curses and slurs uttered, *blood savage, lord of demons, oppressor of Night*. Their fury is palpable, and I can't blame any of them. No one but Zara knows the full truth, understands why I've done what I've done.

We reach the place where the ravine turns sharply, and around the bend I see that it widens. At the end there's an overhang which forms a shallow cave. Within the shadows there, I see three sets of glowing red eyes. Jodin strides beneath the overhang, and I hear the sound of something sliding, a cage door being opened. The crowd fans out behind me, blocking any route of escape.

Jodin reemerges, and at his side walks a monster.

It's a wolf the size of a horse, but instead of fur it has soft, glowing orange spikes running from head to tail. Flames ride on its breath like a dragon. As it inhales and exhales, its body glows like burning coals, as if a fire burns inside it. As a child, I read tales of the fire wolves, but I have never seen one. I am at once awestruck and very much aware of my mortality.

"I am sorry for this," Jaylen says softly. She hangs her head as if my death has already come to pass, and she the executioner.

"You have shown us nothing but kindness," I say. "Do not regret that."

Jodin moves off to the side of the ravine, and his beast stands in the center. Its glowing eyes fixate on me, and it lets out a low growl that shakes my bones.

"Asher!" Zara whispers, her tone laced with desperation.

"Fate will decide. It always does." My eyes meet hers, and there are so many things I want to say, but there isn't time now. So I simply say, "Move back."

I turn to face the wolf.

Jodin utters a command, and the wolf charges me.

I have just enough time to pull my new dagger before the thing lunges for my throat. Rolling forward, I dive beneath its body as it leaps over me, landing in the spot I had been just a moment before. I come out of my roll into a crouch and the thing spins with a ferocious growl. Its molten eyes pin on me and narrow. Then it comes for me again.

This time I can't outmaneuver it. I wrap my hands around its neck as it tackles me. The hand which holds the dagger sinks the blade into the wolf's neck, but it doesn't even flinch. It doesn't bleed, either. I land hard on my back. The beast snaps its teeth at my face, but I manage to hold it far enough away from me to keep it from feasting on my flesh.

It is made of heat and flame, but so am I. I am blood drinker and demon both, and there isn't a blaze that can burn me. That part of me that burns with hellfire feels a strange kinship to this creature, even as it snarls and thrusts for my face, trying to get its jaws around my skull.

With a push of magic to enhance my strength, I hurl the thing backwards off of me. It lands on its side and skids across the floor of the ravine a few feet. The crowd gasps and boos in disappointment, and a few feet away, I hear an angry grunt from Jodin. It's clear who the crowd favorite is here.

The fire wolf leaps to its feet and runs at me again. This time I charge as well and we meet in the center of the ravine in a crash of flame and magic. We fall to our sides, the wolf snapping at my neck and slicing at me with its blade-sharp claws. I hiss in pain as one of its paws opens a gash down the side of my chest. Another few moments and I'm going to be disemboweled.

I send a pulse of magic into the creature, shoving it away from me long enough to get off the ground. Then I leap around to the other side of it so I'm at its back, arm wrapped around its throat in a chokehold. It snarls and gags and thrashes. Within moments, it manages to wiggle from my grasp and leap to its feet.

Crouching again, I face it, realizing that in the struggle I've lost my dagger. I can see it glittering a few feet away amidst the moss. Too far to reach, not that it's going to help me anyway. We face each other, the wolf and I, both breathing heavily. Behind us, the other two wolves still in the cage growl and yip. Its eyes are locked on mine and we appraise each other for several moments.

I don't want to kill this beast, this regal creature of flame and ash. It has no stake in this challenge. It has no vendetta against me. It's only following the orders of its master, a man who keeps a being of legend and fable locked in a cage when it should be running free. We are the same at our core, the wolf and I.

It blinks and cocks its head to the side, and I realize with a wave of shock that somehow the creature understands me. Maybe not my thoughts, but the feelings behind them. We do share a connection. Fellow monsters wrought of fire and ash and magic.

And then, the wolf relaxes its stance and bows its head to me, a gesture so human it sends shivers up my spine.

The other wolves and the crowd in the ravine fall dead silent. Jodin is standing across from me, shock evident in his slack jaw and wide eyes. After a moment, he shakes his head as if he thinks he's dreaming. He points at me and utters the attack command again. But the fire wolf doesn't look at him. He walks to my side and sits down beside me.

"What dark magic is this?!" Jodin bellows. "I demand a life for a life! I will have your head!"

Murmurs move through the crowd, sounds of awe, not curses and taunts as before.

"Nothing like this has ever happened before," calls Elden.

"The battle is over, Jodin," another woman calls. "It was fought honorably. The wolf has spoken."

"But it was to be a fight to the death!" Jodin's face is red-purple with rage, the veins in his neck popping out. "No one is dead! No blood payment was made!"

"Do you wish to challenge the Lord of Night?" Elden asks.

Next to me, the wolf stands again and issues a low growl, its glowing eyes pinned on Jodin.

"As I said before, I do not wish to claim your life," I say softly.

Jodin shakes his head and then strides off beneath the overhang, streaming curses behind him.

"It's time to go," Jaylen says, coming up and touching my arm.

I nod, and we begin to make our way down the ravine. The crowd gives us a wide berth, especially since the enormous wolf walks at my side. I try to look over at Zara, but she won't meet my eyes. I'm afraid I've broken whatever fragile truce existed between us. That burns more than the bloody gash across my ribs, but maybe it's better this way. Because nothing can change the way things are. The inevitable outcome. My brother will always hang between us, no matter how I feel when I'm lying tangled in her arms.

When we reach the tree, the wolf follows us up the narrow steps. The guards stare in awe as we pass through the hollowed trunk. On the other side, the wolf turns and gazes back through the doorway, a low whine issuing from its throat. And then it lets out an earth-shaking howl.

From far down the ravine, there are two answering howls and a crashing sound, followed by a yell. The other two wolves come tearing up the ravine, up the stairs, and through the tree. The guards stand back, eyes wide with terror.

I incline my head to the wolf as it had done to me. "You have your freedom now. One such as you belongs to no one."

The beast bobs its head, its long fiery tongue lolling out of its mouth. Then it lets out another sky-cracking howl, and it turns and lopes off into the forest, followed by its two pack mates.

"They're going to be talking about this for decades," Jaylen says, shaking her head. "Come on. We need to get through the Waste before dark."

I don't bother asking why. I can only imagine.

"Let me look at your wound first," Zara says, her tone stern and brokering no argument.

She doesn't look at me as she examines it. It's not bleeding much since the wolf's red-hot claws cauterized the cut as it made it. But Zara sends a small bit of magic into it to close it the rest of the way up. Then, without another word, she turns and strides off into the forest. I want to call after her, but I bite my tongue. *It's better this way,* I tell myself again and again.

We trek through the forest a short ways, and then Jaylen leads us down a hole beneath the tangled roots of a tree. A ladder stretches down into the tunnels. I wonder how many entrances there are into this labyrinth beneath the earth, and how long it took to map them all.

The smell of dirt and bones hits my nose when we reach the tunnel floor. Jaylen turns to face me and Zara, speaking in a low whisper. She holds the same small stone she had before, that produces just enough glow to see our immediate surroundings.

"When we traveled in the tunnels briefly before, we weren't actually in the area below the Waste," she says. "Now we are right at the edge of it. And within the Waste is where most of the monsters roam. Once we get beyond the next intersection—" She points into the gloomy distance— "There will be no talking. You must make as little noise as possible, and you will follow any instructions I give you, without question. Do not use magic, as that will attract the beasts."

She pauses, looking at us each in turn. "Are you ready?"

Zara and I both nod, and Jaylen turns and begins heading down the tunnel again. We reach the intersection quickly. Jaylen looks left and right, and then heads straight across. Zara follows her, and I take up the rear.

We've just stepped into the far tunnel when Zara suddenly stiffens and stops walking. Her eyes seem fixed on something ahead of us, something I can't see.

Then her legs buckle beneath her, her eyes roll back in her head, and she falls to the ground.

CHAPTER
TWENTY-NINE

ZARA

At first all I can see is a glowing violet light. Blinding me, wrapping around me, pulsating slightly.

It's also whispering. Calling my name in melodious tones, over and over.

The glow fades slightly and now I can see that it runs in a path, flowing away from me like a river. It tugs at me, as if a strong wind is pushing me from behind, curling around my arms and leading me forward. I take one tentative step, and then another.

I know what it is, because it's the most familiar feeling in the world. The force I see in my mind's eye whenever I summon my power, the presence I feel within Night. The wild magic.

But it's never actually *spoken* to me before.

I take another step along the moving path, but then I feel another presence behind me, a different presence. Not a soft purple glow but a dark specter, a rush of darkness and teeth and black wings.

The voices intensify, calling my name frantically, and at the same time the glowing path begins to fade. I look behind me, heart beating and clawing in my chest, and I can see something coming toward me at great speed. I can't make out details, but I know that I do not want it to reach me. I try to run but it's somehow sucking me toward it, and I can sense in the darkness a great tooth-lined maw, opening to devour me…

Everything around me spins and images flash through my head, too rapid for me to capture.

And then I feel my body jerk, and I am back in the tunnel, Asher holding me in his arms, Jaylen standing over me, face stricken.

"Zara!" Asher gasps as my eyelids flutter open. "What happened?"

"I—I don't know," I say, my breath ragged, chest heaving. Terror is still pulsing through my veins. I whip my head back and forth, looking each way down the tunnel to see if the monster is still hunting me.

"What are you looking at?" Jaylen asks sharply.

"It was like…I was having a dream." I shake my head, trying to explain. "The wild magic was calling to me, but then something dark chased me… dark and ancient and *evil*…"

Asher's brow furrows and his jaw clenches. "You had a vision?"

I nod weakly. My limbs feel weak and a fine tremor moves through them.

"We need to keep moving," Jaylen says. "Get her up. We've lingered here too long."

Asher helps me to my feet and wraps an arm around from the side to support me as we move. I'm too flustered from what just happened to object. In this moment, after the horror of that thing stalking me, I need the feeling of his solid chest against my body, the strength of his arms holding me up. I can forget, just for a few minutes, that this means nothing at all.

We walk for hours and hours in silence. The only light is the weak orb from Jaylen's stone, and in the near-total darkness, my other senses become amplified. I can hear my heart beating, and our footfalls sound like beating drums against the earth. Once, in the distance, I hear the dripping of water from some underground creek or spring. The smell of earth and stone and time becomes so intense it seems to fill my nose and lungs, an almost physical sensation. And on my tongue, I can taste it, too. The taste of stale magic and salt.

Sometimes when we reach an intersection, we continue straight, other times Jaylen leads us left or right. I notice that we avoid the larger passages as much as possible, the ones created by the great wyrms. Was it one of those I saw in my vision? I shudder thinking back on it. Never have I felt such unexplainable fear over something I couldn't even see.

When the earth begins to tremble I look around in

alarm, but Jaylen's expression doesn't change much from the usual grim set of her jaw and sharp glint of her eyes. She simply continues walking down the tunnel, not slowing her pace. I can't help but look behind us, though all I see is midnight black.

We reach an area of the tunnels that is criss-crossed with passages, intersections every few feet. It seems the closer we get to Night, the more tunnels there are. I don't know how Jaylen can possibly keep them all straight in her head, but she moves confidently, never faltering in pace. She leads us on a path that changes frequently, making left turns and then right, zigzagging across the maze beneath the earth.

Then, abruptly, she stops and turns to face me and Asher.

"We are being hunted," she says calmly, her voice barely above a whisper. "I've been trying to lose them in the tunnels, but it's not working."

"Them?" I whisper.

She ignores my question. "We are nearly to Night. In a moment, we're going to run. Do not look back, do not slow down for any reason. We will not win a fight against them, so running is our only chance."

Her eyes flick from me to Asher, and we both nod.

"This tunnel leads straight to Night." She points ahead of us. "Run. Now!"

And we run.

We run with everything we have, and my vision replays before my eyes. Some great beast behind me, teeth and wings and ancient darkness. My heart races and my adrenaline spikes so painfully it feels like blades. My lungs soon feel blade-filled as well, so fast are we moving.

I hear it, then, what my sister had apparently noted long before. A scuttling, like dozens of legs, and a low growling that reverberates through the earth. But I do not look back, I keep running as fast as I can.

We pass an intersecting tunnel, and then another, but we continue straight as Jaylen instructed. She's in the lead with the meager light, Asher and I right behind her, shoulder to shoulder. The noises of pursuit grow behind us; our hunters are gaining ground. But we have to be close to Night now. So close.

Then, in the dim light, I see movement in the intersection ahead of us.

Several huge beasts swarm around the corner, blocking our path.

There are three of them. As large as bears, and they look like bears, too. Except that from out of their spines rise huge spindly legs like spiders which frame their ribcages. Each leg is covered in deadly-looking spikes. Their mouths are full of curved fangs and pinchers like a spider, too.

In the darkness I can't see their eyes, though there is the impression of eyes, a glint here and there off a glassy surface. But even though I can't see them, I can feel the weight of their collective gaze. A low growl emits from their mouths, and their legs chitter up the sides of the tunnel as if in excitement.

Behind us, two more monsters arrive, and they call to each other, a strange sound of triumph in their throats. We're surrounded. Zara pulls both of her daggers, and I see Jaylen pull a long blade that was strapped between her shoulder blades. I pull my axe from its sheath at my waist and I hurl it at the forehead of the thing closest to us.

My blade flies true and hits the monster dead center in the face, embedding into its skull with a bone-crunching thud. The beast falls dead to the tunnel floor, and the other two rear up on their hind legs, roaring, and charge us. I can hear them coming up from behind, too.

I grab Zara's hand and yell for Jaylen to duck. We call on the wild magic and it answers, a blast of violet light pulsating from our joined hands, sending the creatures flying backwards a dozen feet at least. I can't tell if they're dead or just injured, and I don't wait to find out. We run for the exit.

Moving around the writhing bodies of the stunned or dying monsters, we make for Night. But we haven't traveled two steps when more of the things swarm into the tunnel behind us. They seem to be coming from both sides of the intersecting tunnel, at least four more of them. We have no choice but to turn and fight. Our blast of magic was so strong it just about depleted what reserves I had left. Zara looks over at me and shakes her head, clearly she's used hers up, too.

Jaylen yells and charges the things, swinging her blade in a broad arc. Zara and I follow. She ducks and rolls, darting in and out like lightning. I leap over one of the felled beasts and manage to pull my axe out of the skull of the other. Then I turn to face the new arrivals, whirling my axe around my body, hacking into spindly legs and jawbones.

But the monsters are fast, too. One of the spiked legs slices across my shoulder and I let out a yell as searing pain consumes my body. I see Jaylen fall beneath one of them, and Zara dives after her with a scream. My vision blurs a moment, my blood pulsing too fast in my temples. The tunnel shakes and I hear growls and snarls rushing toward us.

More of them are coming. We're going to die here in this labyrinth beneath the earth, footsteps from our home.

Something red and glowing flies across the tunnel before me and tackles the monster standing before me. Another blur of light, then another. The smell of fire and ash hits my nose.

The fire wolves have found us.

Shock and adrenaline pump through my veins and I stagger toward the place where Jaylen and Zara disappeared beneath the monster. There's a wolf atop their attacker, its flaming jaws ripping into the neck of the thing, spewing blood and bile. A moment later the thing falls limp, and the wolf lets out a victorious howl.

The pack leader, the one that I battled, is finishing off another of the spider-beasts. It takes a hit from one of the spiked legs, but it barely flinches. Sparks and ash whoosh from the wound, but it growls and leaps atop the back of the thing, slashing at its head from up high until the creature falls dead on the tunnel floor.

I help Zara and Jaylen to their feet. They're covered in blood and dirt, but they're alive. We stumble toward the end of the tunnel. I can see a metal grate in the shadows ahead, and I realize that the tunnels connect to the sewers beneath the city. It's not locked. I shove it open and let Zara and her sister pass, then I whistle to the wolves. Three pairs of glowing eyes fixate on me from the darkness of the tunnel beyond, and then they pound toward me. I close the grate behind me after they pass.

Jaylen points to the right where there's another path that angles up toward the surface. Zara staggers up it, one or both of her legs clearly injured, and Jaylen is pressing one hand into a shoulder wound like mine. The wolves run ahead of us, lighting the path. Dirt turns to moss which then turns to grass beneath our feet. The tunnel grows smaller, so we have to duck as we move ahead.

The tunnel opens into a wooded park. Another grate covers the entrance, which the wolves have already shoved opened. I see the spire of a church rising directly ahead, the first stars of evening glittering above it. Headstones are dotted amidst the trees, and I realize we're in a small cemetery. The fire wolves stand waiting for us by a large marble mausoleum.

"What sector is this?" I ask Jaylen. What I really want to know is, what enemy's territory do we occupy?

"Angelus," she responds. "But we're just north of the river. Not far from Daemonium territory."

We move slowly through the trees and the headstones, alert for angels. One of Zara's legs seems almost entirely unusable, so I move to her side to help her walk as I had in the tunnels after her vision. This time, however, she shrugs away from me.

"I don't need you," she says, her voice cold and quiet.

Jaylen darts her gaze back to us, but she says nothing of what she heard.

It's better this way, it's better this way... I repeat the mantra in my head over and over. I leave Zara and stride ahead, my fire wolf at my side as I reach the edge of the trees. Pausing, I survey the streets to make sure there are no enemies in sight.

There aren't any angels nearby.

What I see before me, however, is far, far worse.

I step up next to Asher at the edge of the graveyard. He's gone as still as one of the headstones we just passed. When I look out beyond him, my breath leaves my body in one big rush.

The City of Night is burning.

It looks as if the fires of hell have been released, one blazing inferno with barely a building spared. My mind tries to comprehend how a city of stone and metal could burn like this, but then I remember Vyrin's words, how he'd said that when magic failed them, they became expert alchemists. That can be the only explanation for such destruction.

In the distance, on the north side of the city near Ellielle's tower, huge catapults fling fireballs far into the streets beyond, some even landing close to the river, nearly in Daemonium territory. The sky is filled with winged creatures, angels and dragons and huge birds of prey. They dive and blast magic back toward Vyrin's troops. On the ground, warriors clash together with swords and axes and maces.

I'm not sure why I expected anything else but what I see before me now. Vyrin said they'd sent an army through the rift the night before. I suppose the fight for my own life, being hunted by dogs and fae and monsters, had occupied my thoughts entirely. But I never imagined it could be this bad so quickly. The battle couldn't have been going on for more than half a day, and yet a huge section of the northern half of Night is in flames.

"Dark goddess," Asher murmurs, eyes wide.

Next to him, one of the wolves lets out a low whine, and Jaylen makes a gesture of prayer over her heart.

"We've got to rally our forces and join the fight," I say, jaw grinding together. "Asher and I will find the Daemonium. Jaylen, do you think the Factionless will join us?"

She does not look at me when she replies, her eyes fixated on the hellish scene before us. As we watch, a fireball hits one of the dragons in flight and it crashes into a building with a reverberating boom, sending a cloud of dust and ash high into the sky.

"I think that they must," she finally says.

"Okay, then." I touch both her and Asher on the shoulder. "We travel together until we cross the river into Daemonium territory. Though, I have a feeling no one is going to interfere with our journey. After that, we split up, and we gather back at the river in three hours time."

"I'll be hard pressed to reach the south side of the city and return that quickly," Jaylen says.

I nod. "I know. Just as quickly as you can."

She nods, and we begin to move. I realize after a few steps that I'm going to slow everyone down. In my horror at the state of Night, I'd forgotten that one of those spider monsters had stabbed through part of my calf. A groan of frustration rises from my throat.

"I can heal your leg," Jaylen says, moving toward me.

"Don't!" I snap, raising a hand to block her. "The wild magic is too unstable. I can feel it."

"Me, too," Asher says. "It's deteriorated greatly since we left."

Jaylen looks back and forth between the two of us. "You're telling me you two have that much control over the wild magic?" Her eyebrows shoot up dubiously.

"I was its anchor for over two hundred years," Asher says gravely, shaking his head. "And then we discovered your sister could link to it same as I could."

"So, when we lost our magic in the explosion, Night lost that anchor," I say softly.

Jaylen's eyes widen. "Well, how do you get it back? Other than…well…" she drops off.

"We don't know yet." I sigh. "Part of me thought since we've regained partial use of it, that once we stepped foot back in Night, it would all come back."

"I hoped that, too," Asher says, looking at me.

I avoid his gaze. "Until we figure it out, don't use any magic. The city had deadly flares of magic before, even with an anchor. I can't imagine how bad things must be now."

She nods and we continue our trek to the river, which thankfully is a short distance. We see not a single soul on the way, and at the river, none of the Syreni can be seen above the surface. Everyone is either engaged in battle or hiding.

After we cross over via a narrow bridge, much smaller than the one in the central part of the city, Asher points down a street slightly to the east. "There's a stable down this way. A cavalry outpost for my spies."

Within a few blocks we reach it, and when Asher strides through the front door, a huge fire wolf looming at his side, the Daemonium on duty falls to one knee. "My lord. We were told you were dead."

Asher gestures for the man to get up. "Not yet. We need three horses."

"I only have two at the moment, my lord," the warrior says in an apologetic tone.

"Two will suffice. Which one is fastest?"

The warrior leads the way down the aisle of the stable and points out a pure white horse. Asher gestures to Jaylen. "You'll need speed more than we do."

The Daemonium, a fire type with two red horns protruding from his otherwise ordinary forehead, helps us put bridles on both of them. But after he puts a saddle on the white horse for Jaylen, Asher shakes his head. "We have only a short ride. We'll forgo the saddle."

We walk back out onto the street, which is filled with

smoke even though the battle is more than two miles away. Jaylen mounts her horse and gives us a nod farewell, her eyes lingering on mine for a moment. "See you soon, sister," she says, and she gallops off into the dusky night.

Without a word, Asher lifts me onto our horse, a huge bay with a white blaze down the front of its face. Then he turns to his warrior. "I need you to shift to scout duty. Relocate closer to the river. If the battle reaches there, inform me at once."

The warrior nods. "Understood, my lord."

"Are the others still at the palace?" Asher asks.

Another nod.

Asher swings up onto the horse behind me and urges it to move on. I can feel the heat of his body as his chest presses into mine, and his arms brush my sides where he holds the reins on either side of me. His breath tickles my ear from behind. I hate how it affects me, how my heartrate increases and my breathing hitches.

The horse prances beneath us, uneasy because of the three huge wolves circling us, the smoke filling the air, and the distant sound of battle; blasts and screams and resounding booms. At a command from Asher, the horse shoots forward into a gallop. When we reach the end of the street we turn right and head for the Palace of Night. The movement sends pain shooting through my leg, but it's much less than if I were walking on it. Asher leans into me as the horse flies through the streets, one hand on the reins as the other wraps around my waist to hold me in place.

The wolves are streaks of glowing coals and flames against the gray of the city.

It's less than a mile to the palace, and soon we're clattering across the cobblestones of the main courtyard, wolves behind us. A swarm of guards rushes out, but when they see who it is they all drop to the ground, their foreheads pressed to the stones. Helios and Malara come rushing out of the main entrance. They stop dead at the sight of Asher and the wolves, their eyes darting back and forth as if unsure what to address first.

"We thought you were dead!" Malara cries. "When Vyrin's army attacked, we assumed the negotiations had not gone well."

"He sent the army before we even met for negotiations," Asher says, his jaw rolling and his arm tightening around me inadvertently. "He never intended anything but to torture me. Not that I was expecting any different."

"And what are these... things that have followed you?" Helios asks, pointing to the larger of the wolves.

"It appears I made some new friends," Asher says with a small smile.

"I see," Helios says. "Your betrothed called for reinforcements an hour ago. We're preparing to march into battle as we speak."

Betrothed. The word worms up my spine unpleasantly. It's yet another reminder of the fact that Asher and I have no future together.

"It will take all of us. Zara's sister is rallying the Factionless as we speak," Asher says.

Malara and Helios cast me looks of surprise. "Sister?" Malara asks.

I nod. "You've heard of her no doubt. The one known as Falling Star."

"Ahh," Helios says, his expression unreadable as usual.

"It was a surprise to us as well," Asher adds, as if feeling the need to defend me.

He dismounts and helps me down, but my leg buckles and he has to hold on to me from the side.

"I'll send for a healer," Malara says, gesturing to one of the guards.

"No," Asher says. "We don't want to risk anyone with the magic like it is. I'll take care of it." He turns for the door. "Gather everyone in the courtyard. We will march in an hour."

The wolves let out a low whine as Asher leads me into the palace, but he looks back and gestures for them to stay put. We're just entering the main hallway when the ground begins to shake beneath us, rattling the walls and the windows, making the ceiling crack and crumble. I can feel something, like the sky when a storm is forming, pressure building and building and building...

And then a pulse of wild magic blasts across Night.

THIRTY-TWO

ASHER

The surge of wild magic rages across the city. It flings me and Zara into the wall, and in the next room a chandelier crashes to the floor, shattered glass flying everywhere. Outside in the courtyard it looks like lightning striking over and over, but it's not lightning, it's magic, violet and glowing. The whole sky is purple with it.

It passes within sixty seconds, and then the sky returns to dark blue. I hear a cry of alarm from outside and see that two of the guards have fallen dead, victims of the tempestuous magic. My fists clench and my jaw rolls.

We have to stop this.

"Come on," I say to Zara. I pick her up, carrying her toward the stairwell to the upper floors.

"Asher," she growls in protest. "Put me down!"

"This isn't the time for your stubborn heroics." I pin

her even more tightly against me and take the steps two at a time to my suite on the third floor.

When I deposit her in one of the chairs in front of the fireplace in my sitting room, she crosses her arms over her chest and glares at me. "Why are we here?"

I walk to the fire and throw in another log. Bless the staff for keeping it lit while I was gone.

"I told you," I say, turning around, "Your wound needs attending to. And we need to power back up before battle."

The look on her face tells me she'd rather stab me than take off her clothes. "Now that we're back in the city, what makes you think that us joining together won't cause an even more horrific surge of magic?"

"Or, maybe that's exactly what we need to do to get our magic back once and for all, to re-anchor Night." I shrug. "Since we know that sex brings our magic back temporarily outside the borders of this city, now that we've returned, that could be the solution."

Zara gives me a look so deadly it would likely kill any other man. "Okay, then. Take off your clothes. Let's save the city so you don't ever have to look at me again."

When I stand there, staring at her, she stands and slowly strips off her tunic.

"Zara," I say softly. "I don't want any bad blood between us. You know I care for you…"

She responds by closing the distance between us and undoing my belt. She yanks it off with a snap of the leather. "Don't talk, Asher."

I pull off my tunic and toss it on the floor next to hers. "So, we're back to you hating me. Like the first time."

"I won't use my dagger this time." She unbuttons my pants.

"Maybe I liked your dagger," I whisper, dropping to my knees.

I take off her boots and carefully roll her breeches down, peeling the blood-soaked area off her stab wound. She winces slightly, looking up at the ceiling to avoid my gaze. When I have them off, I look up at the length of her, bare and glorious, her raven hair cascading down her back. She's smeared in blood and covered in dirt, and she couldn't be more beautiful.

My lips kiss up the inside of the thigh opposite her injury, and when I reach the soft swirl of hair between her legs, I dart my tongue into her. A small gasp escapes her lips, and she grabs my head with one hand, twisting her fingers into my hair. I pull back and slowly run my tongue up the length of her opening, then swirl it over her clit. Zara gasps and her legs tremble.

I don't feast on her as I had in the forest. I am slow, teasing, tantalizing, tasting every bit of her until she lets out a little whimper. Her fingernails are practically crushing my skull, but I don't move any faster. I take my time, even though the world is burning down around us. *Because* the world is burning down around us.

When she cries out, I grab her ass with both hands and press her hard into my face, thrusting my tongue inside of her and sucking as she bucks against me. Magic surges between us, and a glow envelopes Zara as her climax takes her. After several long moments she falls limp against me.

I stand, picking her up as I do and carrying her over to the fur rug by the fire. I set her down carefully and examine her injured leg. As I'd hoped, the magic has healed it, the skin smooth and flawless except for the dried blood. Her eyes glow with a buzz of magic as I draw my gaze back to hers. I stand and pull my pants off, releasing the trapped length of me which had been straining against my clothes. Zara watches me as I drop to my knees, strad-dling her.

"Do you still hate me?" I bend down and kiss the side of her neck, my cock sliding along her belly.

"Yes," she says, but it comes out breathy, more of a purr than a growl.

I position myself so that just the tip of me enters her, no more than an inch. I rotate my hips, teasing right at her opening. In and out, the tiniest bit deeper each time, then pulling back. "Even now?" I bend and flick my tongue over one of her nipples.

She gasps and arches off the floor, but then she rolls me, flipping herself on top. "Especially now," she growls, and she slides the length of me into her.

A groan escapes my lips as she rolls her hips, grinding along my cock.

"And I told you to stop talking."

She places two fingers in my mouth and picks up her pace atop me, rocking back and forth. I suck on her fingers as she rides me, and I grab her ass with both hands, squeezing the firm flesh in my palms. Magic begins to spark between us, and for the first time in days, I feel the force that is Night beneath the city, feel not just the wild magic, but the source of all that magic.

Maybe I'm right after all…

I sit up abruptly, folding myself up to meet Zara so we're chest to chest. I need her closer to me…*goddess*, I always need her closer to me. To feel her heartbeat against mine, feel her breath on my face. Breath which is coming faster now as she gyrates, a fine trembling beginning in her limbs again as she rides me. I wrap my arms around her back and kiss the side of her neck, smelling her skin and the sheen of sweat forming between us.

A storm of the best kind is unleashing within my body, and the glow of our magic fills the room, putting the fire burning beside us to shame. Night stirs beneath us, a rumble as if acknowledging that we've returned, that we're together as it always seems to desire that we are. Zara was fated for me from the moment she entered my life, and I for her. Maybe I'm a fool to fight it, to obsess over the past.

"Zara!" I groan as she moves even faster, sending wave after wave of ecstasy rolling through my body.

She responds with her own cry as she begins to convulse against me, and I pull her even tighter, letting go of the force building within me, surrendering to the torrent of power and pleasure. Magic pulses across the room as our yells fill the air, and the palace shakes slightly as Night rumbles again beneath us.

As our movements subside, Zara looks down at me, her eyes swimming with emotion. "Asher—"

But she doesn't finish her sentence. Because her head rolls back, her body goes rigid, and she stares straight up at the ceiling, eyes fixated on something I can't see.

THIRTY-THREE

ZARA

his time, the vision moves along more quickly. There is the blinding violet light, the path and the voices leading me, the rush of wings and darkness. My pounding heart and the unexplainable terror of the ancient evil behind me. I can't even see it, but I *know* it is the end of me.

The strange images begin to flicker rapidly before my eyes, but this time they repeat long enough so that I get a sense of what they are. Three images, over and over and over…

"Zara!"

Asher is shaking me, hands on either side of my face, panic written in his features. When I straighten and focus my eyes on him, he wraps his arms around me, burying his face in my neck.

"Thank the dark goddess…"

He kisses my neck, my jawline, my lips, lingering

215

there. A sphere of magic rolls in the space between our hearts, spinning slowly.

When he pulls back, he frowns. "Another vision?"

I don't answer his question. I'm too fixated by the words he just used. "*Dark goddess…*" I murmur. "I saw…"

Asher stares at me, brows furrowed, waiting for me to continue.

"In the vision," I explain, "The wild magic is pulling me down a path. Something evil is following me. And then I see three images on repeat. Down in the tunnels they moved too fast for me to see. But now…I know what they are."

I take a deep breath to slow the racing of my heart, which is still pounding from the intensity of what I'd seen. What I'd *felt*.

"The first image is a strange pattern of lines made of wild magic. The second is a set of black stairs… they look like obsidian. And the third…"

When I pause for several moments, Asher prompts me. "The third?"

"The third is…" I look up at him, locking gazes. "The third is a goddess."

Asher's eyes widen and he shakes his head. "Do you mean—"

"She has black hair and a black stone in the center of her forehead, and she wears a dress woven of light and magic…a violet dress." My tone is hushed, my words halting. "I think—I think she *is* Night. She is the source of our magic."

"But that—I don't understand," Asher says.

"I don't either. All I know is that the wild magic—*she* —wants me to find her, before that thing does. That thing of wings and teeth and darkness." I shiver.

"Did the vision show you where she is?"

I shake my head. "Not exactly. But I think I've always known... I just didn't realize how literal it was. When I call on my magic, I feel it beneath the city... I think she is trapped there. Underground."

Asher is silent a moment. "If she's trapped, then that means..." His eyes widen in horror and then he places his face in his hands.

"That she's been trapped since the day you accidentally summoned all the magic," I say softly. "Over two centuries ago."

Asher lifts me off of him, setting me upright on the floor and walking away. He strides into the corner of the room and stands there, arms braced against the wall, head down, clearly deep in thought. I give him a couple of minutes before I approach.

"I've never felt malevolence from Night," I say softly behind him. "Never felt that the wild magic was wicked or vengeful. She must know what you did was an accident."

He doesn't answer me for a long time. When he finally speaks, he says, "I've always known I can never atone for what I did. Not fully. But now? This?"

I rest my hand on his shoulder and slowly turn him around to face me. "You *can* atone. You can help me find her. She clearly needs both of us to release her. She brought us together for that reason."

Asher's eyes search mine. "So, you're telling me the way I feel about you is nothing but the will of a goddess? And once we free her, our purpose together is complete?"

My chest tightens painfully, and I have to force words from my throat. "You should be relieved. You've wanted to walk away ever since you found out where I came from. This should make your choice even easier."

He nods, and just that simple gesture sends a spike through my heart.

"We don't have full access to our magic, though," he says with a frown. He lifts one hand, calls magic into his palm and watches as it runs up his arm. "It's the strongest it's been since the explosion, but it's still not all of it. I don't understand…"

"I don't either," I say. "But we know now what we need to do."

"How are you going to find her, though? An obsidian staircase… that's not much to go on." He frowns.

I take a deep breath and call on my magic. I feel that force that is Night, that violet expanse beneath the city. Knowing now where it comes from sends a shiver of awe along my collarbone. I don't try to send the magic anywhere, or do anything with it like I usually do. No bending shadows, no blasts of battle magic. I just hold it, and I see Night within my mind's eye.

And as I'd hoped I would, as my instincts told me I

would, I feel a tug in my belly, and there's a flare of light on the map of the city that I see in my head.

My heart sinks.

"Angelus sector," I say softly. "She's somewhere beneath there, in the area near Ellielle's tower."

THIRTY-FOUR

ASHER

I let out a low growl. "Right in the midst of the battle. Of course that's where the goddess is."

"We were going to join the battle either way," Zara says. "Apparently fate is drawing us there, one way or another."

"I'm getting a little tired of fate dictating my life."

I walk over to the fire and stare into its flickering depths. I want to tell Zara she's wrong, that her visions are crazy, that there's no actual dark goddess beneath the city who's been controlling our lives. But I've lived as the anchor of the source of that wild magic for over two hundred years. I know in my heart that what she says is true. It seems so *right*, so obvious, that part of me must have known this whole time. Some instinct, some inner truth.

And Zara is right about us, too. This should make things easy. Should erase all of my conflict. Night—the goddess—chose Zara for some reason, brought us together and set the wheels in motion for everything that's happened. I don't have to worry any longer about being in love with my hated brother's protégé, the one he sent to kill me. Once the goddess gets what she wants, I won't feel this way anymore.

"What will we tell the others?" Zara asks from across the room.

"I will tell Malara and Helios that we have a crucial mission to rebalance the magic of Night. We will ride into battle with the warriors—no one else needs to know that we have a different goal. The less who know, the better, in case anyone is captured by the enemy."

Zara nods. "Are you ready, then?"

Her eyes hook onto mine, and I can see the flames of the fireplace shimmering there. She'd put her clothes back on while I stood before the fire, and she looks utterly deadly and dangerous as she slides her daggers into place along her thigh, her face stern and fierce. She is shadow and death and wild magic; she is the song of Night.

I close the distance between us and crush her against me, my lips devouring hers, my tongue claiming her mouth. I want to taste her heat and her passion, I want to feel that spark of power between us before everything changes. One last moment that is ours, and ours alone. Something that fate cannot contrive, something that belongs to me, to *us*.

When I pull back, I run my hand through her hair, cupping her cheek in my palm. Her eyes glimmer with tears, her face filled with such sorrow it cuts me like a knife.

"It's not time to say farewell quite yet," she whispers.

"Just in case, then," I say softly. "In case we don't get a chance to say it later."

She nods and steps away from me. I dress quickly, and we head down to the courtyard to ride to war.

THIRTY-FIVE

The scout we'd left near the river comes running up to the palace gates as we begin to ride out.

"The enemy has pushed us back to the river!" he shouts.

Asher's face is grim as he nods. Malara and Helios ride at his left, and I ride at his right. I look north, and I can see fires burning even from this distance, can hear the cacophony of battle. The horse I'm riding prances anxiously beneath me.

It's been nearly three hours. I turn and look south, wondering how Jaylen has fared in rallying the Faction-less. Asher's three wolves growl and stalk around us, their coats glowing in the darkness. A halfmoon has just risen above the swirling mist of the Waste.

The fact that Vyrin's army has reached the river means that much further Asher and I have to travel through a swarming battle, as if things weren't looking grim enough already. But the odds have always been nearly impossible. If we see another dawn, it will be a miracle. And that miracle won't be delivered by any deity, because I know now that there *is* a higher power, and we're the ones who have to rescue *her*.

Asher signals the warriors and we begin to move toward the river, toward the battle that will decide all. A thousand strong, fighting for survival. We'd done this just three days before, thinking then we faced the battle of our lives. Little did any of us know how much worse things could get. The irony is that it took an even greater enemy to make us finally join forces and quit fighting amongst ourselves.

When we reach the river, it looks as if we've reached the gates of Hell. Seeing it from a distance had been horrifying enough. But now, standing at the edge of the destruction…

The entire northern half of Night is burning, as far as I can see in either direction. The catapults have advanced further south, and as I watch, one of them flings a fireball that arcs over the river and hits a stone church on the other side, in Daemonium territory. Flames encompass the building in a matter of seconds. It is no ordinary fire, as I'd suspected earlier. Only fae alchemy could make something burn so quickly.

Dragons and angels and other winged creatures still dive amongst the flames, blasting magic or shooting arrows or throwing spears at Vyrin's warriors. The enemy seems impervious to the flames—more trickery, no doubt.

They wear a strange black metallic armor, and some ride the enormous bronze horses, who are also fitted with battle armor. With power over the elements like this, I don't know why Vyrin is so thirsty for magic. Except, of course, that no power-hungry maniac can ever be satiated.

Beyond the river, Animus warriors without wings fight on foot. Those who take the shape of wolves or bears or lions or panthers, those with teeth and claws like blades. The Incantrix fight on foot as well, hurling magic and casting deadly spells on the enemy, though they are more at risk than any other, since they not only face attacks from their enemy, but from surges of the unstable magic as well.

The Syreni have risen from the river also. The surface of the water is thick with them, and they summon great waves and cyclones of water which they send through the air to blast back the enemy, or to put out the fires closest to the riverbank. Their tritons are hurled at anyone wearing black armor who approaches the edge of the water.

Screams and roars ring through the air, and corpses litter the ground. At the frontline of battle, so much smoke fills the air that the moon and sky can't even be seen. It's a nightmare of blood and flame and black death. Asher looks over at me, expression grim, and he raises his hand to signal the charge.

As he does, the grates set in the street along the river fly open, and Factionless begin to pour out from below. Incantrix, Animus, Daemonium, Angelus. All the beings of Night, those who forsook their houses, the rebels and the outcasts. They rise from the tunnels below to join the fight for our city.

Jaylen is one of the first, and she gives me a sharp nod as our eyes meet. If I die tonight, if nothing else I am glad to have had just a little time with my sister before I leave this earth. To heal the wound I've carried for the last decade.

Asher salutes her, and then he gives his command. The charge begins.

THIRTY-SIX

ASHER

I ride across the bridge, Zara at my side. There is such a sense of déjà vu. We rode into battle only days before, just like this.

But at the same time, nothing like this.

Because after that, everything changed.

A lifetime seems to have passed since that other battle, and here we are again, fighting for the survival of Night.

We don't combine our magic as we had before to blast our way through enemy ranks, because we don't know how much we're going to need for the mission ahead. How long it's going to last this time before it runs out. Sword and axe aid us now as we cut our way through our foes.

But our foes are not the Angelus and Animus this time. On the other side of the river, the warriors of Night are already engaged in combat with Vyrin's forces, so we do not meet the headlong rush that we encountered previously. The Daemonium and Factionless rush out behind us to bolster against the enemy drive, and Zara and I push forward, moving between warriors locked in combat and dodging fireballs from the catapults. My wolves take care of any who are foolish enough to rush us.

We reach the far side of the courtyard within a quarter hour and push past the main crush of battle. There are few warriors beyond, other than those manning the catapults far in the distance. The buildings around us are all aflame, the air thick with the scent of smoke and burning flesh. My demon side enables me to bear it, but I hear Zara choke, her eyes watering from the heat and smoke.

"Let's dismount!" I call over the noise, and she follows suit as I climb off my horse.

It's slightly more bearable closer to the ground, and we slap our horses on the hindquarters and send them galloping back over the bridge to safety. My wolves growl and crouch down at the sight of fleeing prey, jowls dripping in anticipation, but I shake my head firmly and they do not follow.

The path ahead is clear. But where is Vyrin?

Zara staggers ahead, one of my wolves at her side. She's heading for Ellielle's tower, and I feel her call to her magic, using it as a compass to guide us. I follow her as she picks up a jog, weaving through the smoke and the burning buildings.

The tower rises in the distance, not far now. As we get closer, Zara cuts slightly west. We move around the inferno of a cluster of burning buildings, and she points across a wide courtyard to a church on the far side. It's burning, like the rest of the buildings. I should be able to shield Zara long enough to find a tunnel leading below it. I'll have to trust her magic and her vision to guide us.

She's most of the way across the courtyard when there's a great rush of wind overhead, and the smoke cyclones around us. With a resounding boom, a golden dragon lands in front of us.

Kieran.

He shifts from beast to man in a shimmer of magic, his eyes glowing in the darkness. My wolves let out a chorus of low growls, and Zara pulls one of her daggers.

"What are you doing here, brother?" I call, stepping forward to stand beside Zara. "We have a truce between our houses, remember?"

A smile plays over Kieran's lips. "A truce brought about by your betrothal to Ellielle," he says. "And judging by the magic intertwined between the two of you, it does not seem you have any intention of upholding your end of the bargain." He points a finger and makes a spiral gesture back and forth between the two of us. "It seems you've forgiven our Zara. *Several* times."

"Ellielle has no illusions to any romance between us," I snarl. "It was a move to unify our people and save our home. Now step aside, Zara and I have something we must do."

"I'm afraid plans have changed," Kieran says. "Because Vyrin has offered a different deal. Anyone who brings *her* to him will be spared, along with their house."

He stabs a finger toward Zara.

"First I loved you, then my brother loved you, now Vyrin is obsessed with you…" Kieran shakes his head and lets out an unpleasant laugh. "What is it about you, Zara, that makes everyone lose their minds?"

"You're not taking me anywhere," Zara growls. "You are vastly outnumbered."

The wolves step up beside us, crouched low, teeth gleaming in the night, breath flickering with flame.

Kieran lunges for Zara, shifting as he goes. Wings flare out, clawed hands dive for her shoulders. He spins and bowls me and the wolves over with one wing and we sprawl across the stone tiles beneath us. I summon my magic, but as I do so, the earth shudders violently beneath me.

And then it opens up and swallows me whole.

CHAPTER
THIRTY-SEVEN

Zara

I watch in horror as I'm yanked backwards into the sky. Asher's name pours from my lips, a scream that hangs in the air. Everything moves slowly as if time has paused.

The stone tiles of the courtyard crumble as an earthquake rips across Night.

A massive split opens in the earth.

Asher and the wolves tumble down into utter darkness, falling until I can't see the glow of their flames anymore.

Then Kieran spins in the sky, his enormous wings beating the air as he carries us toward Ellielle's tower.

It's the one building not burning. As Kieran swoops down toward it, I catch a glimpse of the moon before we dive back down into the smoke. The top of the tower has been blown clean off, whether by magic or some explosion, I'm not sure. Kieran hovers over the center of it, where two figures stand below us. Then he drops me, and I land right at the feet of Vyrin and Ellielle. He shifts and drops to the floor in a crouch beside me.

"Well," Vyrin says with a smile for Kieran. "That's much better than fighting to an inevitable death, now isn't it?"

I climb to my feet, my body protesting after being dropped on the hard stone floor. My heart climbs into my chest as I stare up at Vyrin. Because Vyrin is *thrumming* with magic. So much magic he burns brighter than the whole city aflame.

"How did you get so much magic?" I whisper, eyes widening with horror.

Vyrin's sadistic smile widens. "Kieran wasn't the first one here to strike a deal. Ellielle offered me a vast store of magic she'd trapped conveniently inside an orb, just waiting to be absorbed."

I turn to the angel, my mouth dropping open. "You absolute fool. You had a second weapon?"

I see it now, off to the side of the room, a pile of shattered glass. That's what caused the earthquake that cracked the earth. Vyrin breaking open an orb of trapped magic and siphoning it all. It hadn't been a random surge of wild magic at all.

"Of course I had a backup," Ellielle scoffs, though

there's a slight flicker of unease in her eyes as she stands beside Vyrin. "I will do anything to protect my people."

"Including siding with the greatest enemy we've ever known." I shake my head in disgust.

"There was no winning against him, Zara," Kieran says. "Surely you can see that."

"But together..." Ellielle's eyes bore into me. "Together we can assure peace for our houses."

"You are both insane if you think there will ever be peace," I whisper.

"I confess, I'm surprised you survived," Ellielle says, a soft hiss in her voice. "I figured it certain that Asher would kill you in his blood lust during the voyage across the Waste." She shrugs and the smile she casts me glitters with malice. "Hopefully you enjoyed your time with my betrothed. Although I suppose now that Vyrin has spared House Angelus, I don't need Asher anymore."

"You needn't concern yourself with either of them," Vyrin says to Ellielle, his tone laced with warning. He swings his gaze to me. "I have *great* plans for the former Lord of Night. And for you, Zara. You especially. Plans that will take you far from this battle."

A shiver of revulsion climbs my spine and I eye him warily. He has far too much magic for me to attack him, he would crush me in an instant. My hand goes to my dagger nonetheless. I only have one left, the other I'd dropped when Kieran yanked me from the courtyard. But though I'm in grave peril, what I keep thinking of, keep seeing in my mind's eye, is Asher falling beneath the earth. Could he survive a fall like that? Could anyone? Panic crushes my heart in my chest.

Vyrin gestures for Kieran to take me, and Kieran grabs my shoulder and ushers me away from the center of the tower floor. I throw his hand off of me, but he just smiles. We step back against the wall opposite Vyrin.

"Does he know who you really are?" I whisper to Kieran. "Son of the enemy he hated so much?"

Kieran's cheek twitches. "I guess that's the benefit of being youngest, always playing second fiddle. No one ever noticed me, and so no one remembers me now."

I let out a growl. "A lifetime of hatred, all because Asher was born first. Something he had no control over."

Kieran turns abruptly, wrapping his hand around my throat and pinning me to the wall. His fingers crush down on my windpipe. "Do not speak to me of my brother. You know *nothing* of my life."

My dagger is in my hand and pressing into the base of his ribcage, right beneath the bone, before he can draw another breath. "I once thought you had honor. Courage. Compassion. Choosing Vyrin will be your final legacy. Remember that."

Further argument is forestalled by a rush of magic and shadows into the tower. Kieran and I step apart, eyes to the sky, where smoke begins to swirl overhead. Vyrin is glowing with a violet light as he summons the wild magic, even his eyes burn with it. The light of the moon and the torches around the room are consumed as an unnatural darkness spins around him.

Whispering voices ride the shadows, cold voices that cut like blades as they slide past. The blackness that circles Vyrin is thick and darker than the night. I can barely see anything through it, other than the purple glow coming off Vyrin, the pulse of incredible power. All the power he consumed, all if it being thrown into this summons, because he is clearly calling something forth.

Terror works its way up my spine as the deep dark spins around Vyrin, faster and faster. Overhead, lightning crackles in the sky and a resounding clap of thunder shakes the entire tower. The power in the room builds to a terrible crescendo, the strength of it crushing the breath from my lungs, pressing me back against the wall, pinned in place.

I know what he is summoning, because I've felt it before.

The storm within the tower stops abruptly, the spinning ceases, and a looming darkness shivers into place before Vyrin. A spot of blacker black amidst the dark room, a presence without a body. It rotates once, observing the room and its contents.

And then it lunges, rushing into Ellielle's body.

She screams as it punches through her ribcage, a short cry which cuts off a moment later. Then the darkness expands within the body that was formerly hers, flaring out wings that have turned from blue to black. It grows in size, flesh morphing, bones snapping, until it resembles nothing of the angel that stood there moments before. It is darkness and teeth and claws and wings.

It is the thing that hunts me in my visions.

THIRTY-EIGHT

Zara

The winged darkness turns and its eyes fixate on me. Eyes that glow a deep blue like the previous owner of its body, though not much else resembles her now. A low growl vibrates across the room, a sound of *hunger*.

"Well," Vyrin says, looking up at the beast in awe, "Ellielle did say she would do anything for her people. We all have a price to pay."

"That includes you," I snarl, despite the fear that threatens to choke me.

"One day, no doubt," Vyrin says, unperturbed. "But not today."

Kieran stands rigid at my side, completely silent. His

wide eyes tell me he knew nothing of Vyrin's plan to summon this thing.

"For such a *very* long time I've waited for this day…" Vyrin closes his eyes a moment in apparent bliss. "The day my magic returned to me. The day I crushed my enemy and took my revenge. So long I waited, and while I waited, I planned. And I *listened.*"

His eyes flick up to the creature, the ancient demon at his side. The susurration of its wings makes me shiver.

"In my dreams the darkness spoke to me, and it told me this day would come. And it told me what I needed to do." Vyrin's eyes lock onto mine. "Wait for the woman with purple eyes and raven hair, the one who arrives through the mist. The one who tamed the heart of a monster."

Vyrin's gaze pivots to Kieran. "Not one monster, but two."

When Kieran stiffens, Vyrin lets out a low laugh. "Yes, second son. I know of you, too. The beast told me a great many things."

"One thing remains to be done now…" Vyrin continues. "I have reclaimed my magic and I have summoned forth the beast, but we are not done. One final step is needed for me to become the most powerful being in existence, to secure my dominion for all time. After this day, I will have the magic I need to rule this entire world, from shore to shore. All of Aureon will bow to me."

The horror of his words presses in around me, crawling over my skin and racing in my pulse. It had been horrific enough thinking of Vyrin taking over Night. But the ruler of all? A darkness consuming this entire world?

"You, Zara," he continues, glowing eyes holding mine. "You will lead us to the source of Night."

His words snap me from my spiral of fear. "Why do you need her?" I growl. "You have more than enough magic already. More magic than anyone."

"That is true. But if I leave the source of magic for others to summon, I leave myself open to attack for the rest of my days." Vyrin smiles. "I don't just want the most magic. I want *all* magic. All magic, so that no one can one day unseat me."

"I won't help you." I spit on the tiles of the tower floor. "Go burn in the hell you've created."

Vyrin only smiles. "I knew you would say that."

He raises a hand. Magic flares out from his fingertips and agony lances through my body, an agony unlike anything I've ever known. It feels like I'm being ripped apart from the inside, a million points of pain, my blood and my bones disintegrated.

My consciousness slips away.

———

When I come to, I am slung over Kieran's shoulder. He's walking down a tunnel. It is dark except for two purple orbs of magic that float on either side of him. I can see the slim, shadowy figure of Vyrin walking a few steps ahead.

Which means...

My heart climbs into my throat and I thrash when I feel the weight of the shadow demon's eyes on me from where he walks directly behind Kieran. The cold touch of his dark, ancient magic makes everything in my body scream.

Kieran deposits me unceremoniously onto the floor of the tunnel. I push up onto my elbows and glare at him. "She's awake," he says.

"I can see that," Vyrin says in an oily tone. He pauses only a moment, then continues walking. "It's time to get to work, Zara. Lead us to the source of Night's magic. Unless you want my pet to take a little taste of you…"

The winged beast's mouth widens unnaturally as its jaw unhinges and it reveals rows of gleaming teeth, long and thin like knitting needles. I scramble backwards away from it. I'll have to play along for now, until I can think of something…

I climb to my feet and stride ahead of Vyrin. "I need to use my magic to see the path," I say in warning before summoning a ball of purple light into my hands.

"I'm glad you can be agreeable," Vyrin says with a smug sneer.

Kieran narrows his eyes as he watches me, but he says nothing.

I focus on my magic as I had before, not sending it anywhere but just sensing Night and the glow of magic within the city. We're beneath the church I'd been heading to when Kieran intercepted me. Intercepted *us*. My throat tightens, but I shove away thoughts of Asher and whether he's alive.

Kieran must have told them where we were headed, and they'd clearly found their way into the tunnels beneath the city. The tug I now feel isn't north, south, east, or west, it's *down*. I picture the obsidian stairs in my head. Somewhere below us, that's where the goddess is trapped. Somewhere very deep beneath the earth. Do the tunnels even lead that far?

But right now, it doesn't matter. Because I have no intention of leading them in the right direction.

The sparks of an idea begin to form in my head. A terrible, reckless, dangerous idea. An idea formed of desperation.

"This way," I say, and we continue down the path, heading west, away from the church.

THIRTY-NINE

Asher

I awake in total darkness to the sound of howls of mourning.

My eyes blink open and at first I think I'm blinded, because I can't see anything. My entire body is one massive point of pain. Moving slowly, I roll over just enough to see the soft glow from two of the wolves a dozen paces off. They're standing over the body of the third. It must have snapped its neck in the fall. The pack leader and the other both roll back their heads and let out slow, resonant howls that echo through the air.

I have no idea where I am.

Memory surges back then, asserting itself over the peril of my situation. Kieran has Zara. He's taken her to Vyrin. I can still hear my name, ripped from her throat as he carried her off into the night sky.

Thoughts of vengeance and murder pulse red behind my eyes, but I'm in no position to swear to avenge Zara. I can barely move, and my leg is most definitely broken. Not clean through, but fractured for sure. It feels like a hot poker being shoved into my knee every time I try to sit up.

Slowly, my eyes adjust to the darkness. The glow from the wolves helps a bit, too. Gradually, the outline of rocks appears in the distance, boulders really. Some that form spikes at the top. It smells of water and clay. I must be in a cavern beneath Night. Deeper even than the tunnels we traversed.

I finally manage to sit up, biting through the agony that lances my body as I do. Had I not been Daemonium, I would not have survived such a fall. But even so, I'm lucky. We are not immortal, after all. Not entirely.

Summoning my magic, I send a bit into my leg, enough to heal the fracture. I climb to my feet and walk to where the wolves stand over their fallen friend. The leader looks up at me with sorrow in his glowing eyes, flames flickering from his mouth. Anyone who ever said that animals do not feel the same depth of emotion as people is a fool.

I call magic again, a ball of it in my hand so I can see my way around. I send it high above my head, feeding it more energy, enough to illuminate the cave around me in a soft lavender glow. Turning this way and that, I try to ascertain if there's any way out of this place. Other than the hole in the earth I fell from.

The cavern seems to have solid walls on all sides but one. That side continues further than my light reveals. I pull the ball of magic back to me to conserve it, dimming it so I have enough to guide my way only. Then I begin to walk.

I reach the end of the cavern in less than five minutes. It intersects with a tunnel that runs both ways as far as I can see. But there's also something that continues on the other side of the tunnel.

A set of obsidian steps leading down into darkness.

My heart beats so fast in my chest it feels like it's going to bruise itself. Zara's vision. The stairway. The goddess.

With trembling hands, I hold my light aloft and descend the smooth black steps. They are wide, spanning about a dozen feet on each side of me, and deep, as if made for the feet of giants. They are not, however, very long. Eleven steps, and then I reach the bottom.

A massive stone temple stretches before me. It is made of obsidian, too, floor, pillars, and ceiling. As I step forward into it, torches along the walls burst to life, torches set in glass holders shaped like crescent moons. It is not natural flame that lights them but magic, flickering violet orbs of it. I can taste the magic on my tongue, ancient and reminiscent of stars.

I walk the length of the temple, and at the end stands a simple throne made of stone, with straight, clean lines and a back that forms a triangle at the top. There are no carvings, no adornments.

It is also empty.

I turn in a circle, lifting my light high, sending more magic into it to brighten the room, to make sure I am not somehow missing the obvious.

But there is nothing to be seen. There is no one here.

The goddess Zara saw in her vision is gone.

Zara

I can tell when we reach the edge of the Waste by the change in the air. The tunnels smell of earth and bone, but they also smell of old magic, remnants of the blast two centuries ago that created this place.

I'd been using the location of the goddess to guide me here, moving away from her instead of toward her. Keeping a ball of magic palmed in my hand, seeing the layout of Night in my head, and putting distance between me and that bright light that lies at its source.

"Are we close now?" Vyrin asks, his tone a mixture of suspicion and eagerness.

I know he must sense the old magic, same as me. "Yes,

He nods, eyes bright.

Behind me, Kieran remains silent, and I don't dare look back at the thing of shadows and teeth. I'd been terrified from the moment I began to move away from the goddess that it would be able to sense my deception, or somehow know we were going in the wrong direction. But it must not be able to sense her, or else they wouldn't need me. I'd be locked in a cell, or dead.

So far, my plan is working. But the hardest part lies ahead. The part that will likely get me killed.

I brighten the flare of my magic slightly when we reach an intersection of the tunnels, making a show of using it to look down each. We're slightly north of where we entered Night with Jaylen just hours before, and as I'd suspected, this area is just as criss-crossed with a multitude of tunnels as the place we'd crossed. I take several turns until I find one of the wider tunnels, and I turn down it.

"Almost there!" I call, loud enough so that my voice echoes down the tunnel.

We continue walking for several minutes, though it seems an eternity. My heart beats so loudly I'm sure the others can hear it, and my throat is tight and dry. I slowly bleed more magic into the ball of light at my fingertips, brightening it gradually.

When the tunnels begin to shake, I can't tell for a moment which direction it's coming from.

"What is that?" Vyrin asks, eyes flaring wide.

I spin, looking both ahead of us and behind. I'm so distracted by whatever is coming that when I stumble into the next intersection, it takes me a moment to realize the tunnel to my right isn't empty.

Isn't empty in the least.

The great wyrm stares at me with milky white eyes, eyes narrowed in a look of patient cunning. It fills the entire circumference of the tunnel, which is a dozen feet high. The rest of its body is white, like its eyes. It is strangely beautiful, like one of the dragons of House Animus, but with a long, serpentine body and no wings. Its front claws are huge, the length of two swords each, and curved in an arc almost like a scythe.

I'm clearly not the only one who set a trap today.

The wyrm opens its huge jaws, revealing a row of deadly dagger-like teeth, and then it lunges.

I dive forward across the intersection and it misses me by a hair, the side of its face knocking into my feet and sending me crashing into the tunnel wall. My vision blurs a moment, and I hear yells of alarm from Vyrin and Kieran. I've landed upside down, so for a moment my perspective is flipped. As I scramble to right myself, the wyrm retracts its head, shaking in fury.

That's when the second wyrm, the one making the tunnel tremble, bursts through the ground near my feet. I fall backwards as it lunges up and over, past the head of the first one, and swallows Vyrin whole.

A mighty roar fills the tunnel as Kieran shifts into dragon form and launches himself at both wyrms. I don't wait to see who wins. I get to my feet, and I run in the opposite direction as fast as I can. The ball of magic in my hand lights the way, and I call on more magic to wrap shadows around me and help me run faster. I can only pray I don't attract more monsters before I get out from under the Waste. Now that Vyrin is gone, no longer buzzing with all that magic like a dinner bell, I'm going to stand out all the more.

I know it's not far—a quarter mile at the most. My plan had worked. But I have no idea what comes next.

Without Asher, I can't free the goddess and fix the magical imbalance. It has to be the two of us together, and I don't know where Asher is, or if he's even alive. For the first time since Kieran carried me off, I allow the sob of sorrow that's been sitting in my chest to break free. I let the tears exit my eyes and fling from my cheeks as I flee.

I don't know what I'm going to do if he's gone. Not just because Night will fall... but because my soul will be broken forever.

When the feeling of old magic fades from the earth, I know I'm back within Night. I sag against the wall for several moments, my lungs burning, my heart beating itself raw against my ribcage. It's in that moment of stillness, with no sound but the beating of my heart and my ragged breath, that I realize I'm not alone.

I can sense it coming up behind me, just as I had in my visions. Darkness and teeth and ancient evil.

Zara

It seems I've been running forever. As if my whole lifetime has led to this flight through darkness, terror pumping in my veins.

The fact that I've experienced it before in my visions only compounds the feeling. Except its different this time. Because in my vision I had not laid eyes on the thing that hunts me, it was only a primal fear of the unseen evil.

But now I know what pursues me. Had seen it break through Ellielle's body and claim it for its own. Had seen its eyes and teeth and dark, dark wings.

My magic is beginning to fail, and then I'll be without light and without the ability to navigate. I will die here in the darkness as the demon feasts on my flesh and my soul.

But I'm so close. I can't fail now. Not when I'm nearly there.

The tunnel widens and grows in height, turning from dirt to stone. A rough-hewn staircase appears on my left, leading down into darkness. I fling myself down it, following it as it spirals deeper beneath the earth. It's no manmade structure, not this far beneath the surface. It was made by the goddess, by Night itself. It must have been.

When the staircase finally ends, a long hallway stretches ahead. Drawing more air into my lungs and calling on the last reserves of my magic, I run. But the rush of wings coming from behind tells me I'm not going to make it. The hairs on the back of my neck sense the monster on my heels.

As it whooshes down on me, I spin and throw the last of my magic at the thing, sliding on my back down the hall. I know I won't kill it, but I'm not going to die without a fight. I will not let fear be the last thing I know in this world. A thin bolt of violet light hits the creature as it emerges from the darkness, teeth first, its gaping maw open wide.

But then a powerful blast of wild magic merges with mine, coming from behind me.

Asher strides out of the darkness, arms raised, roiling with deadly power. He holds nothing back, putting every bit of his magic into the attack. The winged demon flies backward and crashes into the wall. Pulling me to my feet, Asher wraps me in the circle of his arms and we back slowly down the tunnel.

A strange sound issues from the darkness, and as the thing straightens and steps forward, I realize it's laughter. I also realize that though Asher and I are tapped out of magic, I can still see the beast somehow. From some unknown source of light beneath the earth.

Turning slowly, I see to my right a large chamber lit with torches. A chamber that sits at the bottom of a set of obsidian stairs.

I look up into Asher's eyes. We made it. Both of us, against all odds. But we're out of magic, and we've led the winged demon right to the source of Night.

CHAPTER
FORTY-TWO

Asher

I pull out my axe and Zara pulls her remaining dagger. I whistle for my wolves, who are still in the nearby cavern standing vigil for their fallen kin. Even with them we will not win this fight, but we will go out with blades clenched in our fists.

The thing of darkness crouches, claws raised, jaws gleaming, eyes bright with blood lust.

And then there is a mighty roar, a roar that shakes the whole earth, and a golden dragon emerges from the darkness behind the winged terror. It grabs it in its teeth and shakes it like a dog before flinging it down the tunnel away from us.

My brother.

He shifts back into a man only long enough to speak, his glowing eyes pinned to Zara. "*This* will be my legacy," he says. Then he turns to me. "Save Night. Both of you."

That's all he has time to say before shifting back to dragon form and turning to face the ancient darkness once more. They collide with such force that another tremor shakes the tunnels and cracks run up the stone walls.

I stare in horror for a moment, but Zara tugs my hand. "We have to hurry, or we're all doomed."

"I've already looked," I say, shaking my head, despair rushing through me. "The goddess isn't there."

Zara's eyes flare for a moment, and her eyes sweep down the length of the temple. Then she shakes her head. "That's because we weren't here together."

I can only hope she's right. A sharp nod, and we flee down the obsidian steps. My wolves fly past as we do, flame and smoke and ash, joining Kieran in his fight. When we reach the floor of the temple, we run as fast as we can to the throne on the far side.

The throne remains empty, even as we slide to a stop in front of it.

"This is the place, I know it," Zara growls, brow furrowed. "She has to be here."

I look at the empty throne and back to Zara, my heart sinking. "Maybe she requires magic, and we're all out."

Zara shakes her head, jaw clenched, anger etched into her face. "No. It can't end here. Not like this. Not when we came *so* close."

Silence falls between us. The temple shakes as Kieran

and the demon battle a few hundred yards away. My brother finally forgave me, and now he's going to die for nothing…

I take both of Zara's hands and look down at her. "If this is the end, I will not go out a coward. As a stubborn, prideful bastard who didn't speak my heart." My gaze drops, but I force myself to look up again, to meet Zara's eyes. "I'm sorry I was angry. It was wrong of me to begrudge you for your past, especially given mine. I've treated you poorly, shoved you away because of things that seem so unimportant now, here, at the end."

One hand reaches up into her hair, and I stroke her cheek with my thumb. "We may die today, but I will spend a thousand lifetimes proving to you that I'm worthy. I will find you in each one, and I will choose you. Over and over, I will choose *you*. My soul belongs to you, and my heart and my body and my blood. Everything I am is yours. Always."

Zara reaches out and curls my tunic in her fist, pulling me against her. "I don't regret any of the lies I told you in the beginning," she says. "Because I told them to my enemy. But I regret the lie I told you after our first night together. You offered me a seat to rule at your side, and I told you I didn't know what I wanted. The truth is that I want you always, too. I've wanted it since the moment I held that dagger to your throat."

"*Always*. In this life and the rest of them."

I press my lips to hers, wrapping my arms around her, holding her close one last time. Because there's not long left in this life, and it's going to be a very long while until I find her in the next. So I taste her, her lips and her tears and the magic that sings in her soul, and I vow to hold onto this moment until we meet again.

And as I do, magic flares between us, and the temple disappears.

CHAPTER FORTY-THREE

Zara

I blink as the pulse of violet light fades, my heart pounding. We're still in the temple. Or some version of it.

Instead of an obsidian floor, we stand on a field of stars. And instead of a throne made of stone, there is a throne made of something that looks like slices of the moon, fragments of it, fanned out around a glowing silver orb.

On the orb sits a goddess.

She has long black hair within which I can see stars and far-off universes. Her skin seems to change as I look at it, depending on the angle of the light: one moment it seems alabaster, the next moment it nearly matches her hair, the next it is a dusky sunset hue like the evening sky. The spot in the center of her forehead, which I'd previously thought was a small black stone, is actually a tiny spinning vortex. Stardust shimmers in the air around her.

My eyes fly to Asher's and we step away from each other and bow low to the floor.

"Rise, children of Night," she says. Her voice is deep and resonant, and yet somehow soft and musical all at once. "You've done well. Just one final step."

"Yes, anything," Asher says. "I've lived in torment since the day I summoned you. I did not know what would happen, I swear it."

He bows his head, but the goddess just smiles.

"I could feel your anguish as time went on," she says. "Your regret. What's important is that you now return things to the way they are meant to be. Magic rebalanced, returned to the lands beyond your city."

"Just tell us how," I say. "What do we need to do to fix it?"

The goddess cocks her head to the side. "I think you already know. You have seen it."

I shake my head in confusion. "But…" I trail off.

I *do* know.

The first image in my vision, before the obsidian stairs or the goddess. A set of strange glowing lines of wild magic.

I know, without knowing how I know, that they are the lines of wild magic running throughout the whole land, throughout Aureon. And when Asher accidentally summoned too much magic, he altered the pattern, trapping the goddess here and siphoning all the magic into Night.

I realize also what the winged demon wants. Instead of returning the balance, it wants to kill the goddess and devour all magic. It never intended for Vyrin to possess that magic, he was only ever a pawn, and a foolish one to think otherwise. Long had that darkness poisoned his mind, driven him mad lusting for something he would never have.

"Do you know what to do now?" The goddess asks me.

I nod.

"And you understand what you'll be sacrificing?" she prompts.

Asher looks at me, and he nods. He understands somehow, too, even though he didn't see the visions as I did. He looks at the goddess.

"I will give up everything I have. Everything except for the woman at my side."

Another smile. "I brought the two of you together through the wild magic, but I did not make you fall in love. That was your own creation, a beautiful one indeed. I would never ask you to give that up."

"Okay, then," I say, taking Asher's hand. "We're ready."

Another blinding flash of light, except this time, we are the source of it. We are the wild magic. *All* of it.

The temple beneath the earth returns, hard obsidian beneath our feet. The winged darkness is descending the obsidian steps toward us. Kieran lies fallen in the hall behind it, the torchlight flickering on his golden scales. One of the wolves lies dead beside him and the other is injured, trying to get up off the floor. It lets out a low whine.

Hands clasped, we stride for the creature. Magic as bright as the sun and moon together rises within us, all the excess magic that has been trapped in Night for over two centuries. In my mind, I picture the lines of magic across the earth, noting where the pattern got twisted.

Before, I always had to hold back, because to summon all of the magic meant sure death. Even Asher and I together could barely contain the force of it, could barely keep Night and ourselves from being ripped apart. But what we're about to do will require all the magic we can summon, and since there's been so much trapped here for so long, it's enough to destroy—or create—anything. Moving as one—one magic, one mind—Asher and I do two things simultaneously.

We reach into the pattern of the magic and we correct the error, the trapped power.

And we thrust the resultant explosion caused by the magic being freed into the darkness looming before us.

The winged beast dissolves into a million particles of violet dust as it's ripped apart by the force of the escaping magic. A pulse and a resounding tremor run through the temple and all the torches flicker. I can feel it rolling out away from us, magic rushing across the land as the balance is restored. Rushing far away, farther than I ever imagined the world could stretch. And I can feel a hum, a wholeness, like a perfect note of music in a song that hasn't been sung for a very long time.

When the hum fades, so does our magic. All of it, our sacrifice to save Night. To save all of Aureon.

Asher bends and presses his lips to mine. When he pulls back, he says, "It is done. It is right now."

I nod and pull him against me for a moment. Then we walk the long length of the temple. At the top of the stairs, Asher stops and stands over Kieran's body for a long while in silence. His wolf, the pack leader, limps to his side and licks his free hand.

"I will send for his body so the Animus can give him a proper farewell," he says at last.

It takes us a long while to find our way out of the tunnels and back to the surface. When we finally emerge, the first light of dawn streaks the horizon. The battle has ceased, and the fires are being put out one by one.

At first, I don't realize what's different. Why the horizon looks so strange.

And then I see.

I see the sun at the horizon, because the Waste is no longer blocking it. The swirling fog is gone, and I can see for miles and miles in all directions. A sigh of wonder escapes my throat.

"Soon, my love," Asher says, pulling me against him. "Soon we will travel beyond this place, and then we will see the whole world."

CHAPTER
FORTY-FOUR

Zara

The sun sets as I climb the path up the side of the mountain, the last rays of it turning the horizon to pink and violet. Deep, dusky violet like magic. Or rather, like the magic that runs through Night. Because I've learned, over the last three moons as Asher and I traveled Aureon, that in other places the magic is a different color. A different smell, a different taste. Now that it's been rebalanced and returned to the world, I've seen many, many different expressions of magic, each one wondrous and unique.

Seen, observed, but never used.

And even though there's a part of me that feels sorrow for the loss of my magic, that connection to my home and the earth that runs beneath it, there's a much bigger part of me that rejoices. Because the war is finally over, the war that waged centuries. There is peace and there is freedom and there is hope.

We've seen it everywhere we've gone, and where there is injustice, or people trying to misuse magic, we've addressed that, too. Jaylen sends us regular updates from Night, where she was elected to rule while the city rebuilds. Cyrena elected a new leader for themselves also and appears to have turned a new leaf in their sordid history. We'd visited there first, to reclaim the horses we'd had to leave when we fled, and to ensure that without Vyrin they would choose peace over war.

We'll go back home one day, once we have seen our fill of the world that we were shut off from for so very long. I know I can't stay away forever, because part of my soul still belongs there.

By the time I reach our camp on a cliff overlooking a valley of rolling green hills and snow-peaked mountains, night has fallen and stars have claimed the sky, burning holes in the velvety canvas. A full moon is rising, painting everything in a silvery glow. I have a satchel of supplies from the village below, including a bottle of honey-oak wine I plan to surprise Asher with.

But as I come around the boulder that serves as the entrance to our makeshift home, I stop dead in my tracks.

The cauldron over the fire is kicked over, the bedrolls are strewn about, and there are scuff marks all across the dirt. Asher is nowhere to be seen.

My dagger is in my hand in an instant and I crouch into a battle stance, ready for attack. Slowly, I move forward, my steps silent. I may not be able to bend shadows anymore, but I've never really needed them to disappear.

I hear my attacker's footsteps from behind a moment before they're on me.

Spinning, I throw out one of my legs to send him sprawling, and in the next instant I'm straddling him, knife at his throat.

"I told you I liked your dagger," he says in his voice of smoke and steel.

I press the blade into his throat even harder, drawing a thin line of blood. "I brought you wine, and this is your idea of a romantic evening?"

In one swift movement, Asher flips me so he's on top, grabbing my wrists and pinning them over my head. He bends close to my neck so his words tickle my ear, his breath hot against my skin. "Tell me you don't like it and I'll release you."

"As if you could hold me," I taunt.

I wrap my legs around his waist, feeling him grow hard against me. I buck my hips up and a low rumble moves through his chest. While he's distracted, I flip him again, rolling him across the grass until we land sitting upright, me straddling his lap. Asher's hands cup my ass cheeks, peeling up the leather skirt I'm wearing.

"To think I lived centuries without knowing such a wondrous article of clothing existed," he says, kissing down the side of my neck. "The Tyrlians really know their fashion."

"Stop talking, Asher," I growl.

He responds, having gotten my skirt up around my hips, by inserting one long finger inside me from behind. A gasp escapes my throat and I shudder against him. He pumps his finger twice more, curling it inside of me until I see stars.

"*Asher*," I moan. "Don't stop…"

He works at his pants with one hand while he continues to penetrate me with the other. And then something much larger than his finger is pressing against my sweet core. He places both hands around my hips and I take the full length of him into me. The sky spins, and Asher moans, burying his face into my neck.

I roll my hips slowly, pulling off his tunic as I do. He pulls off mine and then we are skin to skin, bare beneath the moon and the stars. We lock eyes as I move, picking up the pace slightly. Asher's muscular arms are wrapped around my lower back, and I have one around his neck, one around his back, nails digging into him as pleasure spikes through me.

My lips move to the spot where I nicked his skin with my dagger, and I run my tongue across it. Asher lets out another growl and crushes me even closer against him, thrusting up into me as I gyrate my hips. I cry out and lean back, closing my eyes a moment as I grind against him harder and faster. My climax begins to blossom within me, each petal unfurling in a wave of bliss.

I open my eyes again and bend to kiss Asher as a moan moves through me. Our lips meet, and Asher's eyes fly wide.

"Zara," he says breathily. "Your eyes... they're glowing."

I feel it then, as my pleasure sweeps me away...a rush of magic. Magic that feels like the night sky and the stars overhead and the burning orb of the full moon. A cry rips from my throat, and Asher shudders against me, his own eyes turning molten copper, like flame and blood mixed. He yells and explodes inside me as we're consumed by our ecstasy and the wash of new magic spiraling around us. Violet and vermillion sparks shoot up into the sky.

We collapse on the grass, trembling and clinging to each other.

"What just happened?" Asher says softly, his voice gravelly and rough from the intensity of our lovemaking.

"I think... I think magic found us again," I whisper. "But a new magic. Your eyes have never glowed that color before."

The night hums around us as we lie on the mountain-top, listening to the wind blow and the crickets sing and the sound of our hearts beating.

After a time, we get up, sitting in the grass near the edge of the cliff, fire rekindled behind us. I pour the wine, which luckily didn't get broken when Asher decided to play his little prank. His wolf trots up from a hunting expe-dition, nose bloodied, and lays down in the grass while we pass the bottle back and forth.

"I can't believe you made me think we'd been robbed," I say with a smile. "You're a terrible person."

"And you, my thief and cutthroat, are in no position for judgement."

He makes as if to hand me the wine, but when I grasp the bottle, he yanks me forward into a kiss.

"Don't forget *liar*," I whisper against his lips.

"If you keep that up, you're going to be punished," Asher growls.

"Well then, I'll make sure to be as badly behaved as possible." I kiss him once more, and then I look out across the moon-painted valley. "Do you think we're shirking our responsibility, traveling around like this?"

Asher looks over at me. "We both served our duty and beyond. It was time for a fresh start. I don't think the people of Night will ever view me in a positive light. Besides, your sister makes an excellent leader."

"But surely it can't all be peaceful and happy forever." My brow furrows. "I wonder, sometimes, if Vyrin and the demon are truly gone…"

"You're right," Asher agrees. "There will be darkness again. There will always be evil in the world, waiting for its chance. But when it shows its face, we'll be ready for it."

I summon a ball of magic in the palm of my hand, feeling a stir of wonder in my chest. It feels different than it did before. Light, effervescent. Like pure stardust.

"Yes," I whisper. "If it does, we'll be here."

I let the magic dissipate and I run my fingers along

Asher's jawline, climbing into his lap as I do. "Now. What's a thief have to do around here to…"

"Stop talking, Zara," Asher growls.

And he shows me.

THE END

I hope you enjoyed Zara and Asher's story! The City of Night duology is the first in the connected Crowns of Aureon series. To continue the adventure, read House of Gilded Nightmares next, about Sarielle, a priestess swept off to the Realm of Nightmares to become their queen, and Zyren, the shadow-fae guardian sworn to protect her.

Also, make sure to follow me on TikTok, Instagram, and Facebook, or sign up for my newsletter to get the latest news on my next epic romantasy tale.

If you also like paranormal romance with witches, shifters, and demons (I have a type, what can I say), then binge the Raven Society Series today. Flip the page to read the first three chapters…

XOXO, Aurora

1 HOPE YOU ENJOYED ZARA AND ASHER'S STORY!

I'm just beginning to explore the world of Aureon, so make sure to follow me on TikTok, Instagram, and Facebook, or sign up for my newsletter to get the latest news on my next epic romantasy tale.

If you also like paranormal romance with witches, shifters, and demons (I have a type, what can I say), then binge the Raven Society Series today. Keep flipping to read the first three chapters…

XOXO, Aurora

SNEAK PEEK

Hot Hex:
Raven Society Book 1

CHAPTER ONE

Rowan

My favorite aunt died a week after my divorce was finalized. And here I'd been foolish enough to think nothing could hurt worse than my husband cheating on me. Anger is so much easier than sadness.

Can I also say I'm so over attorneys right now?

I down the double shot of espresso sitting in front of me in one gulp. A frown crosses my lips as I hold my cell phone away from my ear for a moment. "Can you repeat that?"

"Sybil left you everything," says Maria, my aunt's estate attorney. "But there are a few...*complications*."

I really don't like the way she says that word. "Complications?" I get up from the bistro table at the café I'd stopped into. A buzz of nervous energy runs through my fingertips as I grab my purse.

"It would be better if we spoke in person, Rowan." Maria's voice sounds fuzzy coming over the line, as if she's standing in a rainstorm.

Dropping a twenty on the table, I head for the door and out onto the street. I walk in the direction I parked my car. "You know I live in California, right? And you're in what —Massachusetts?"

That's the extra weird thing about all this—I hadn't even known Aunt Sybil had a house in Massachusetts. She'd traveled a lot, had wanderlust in her bones. But she'd always lived close by in California. Or so I'd thought. Now I'm not sure about anything. What other secrets had she been keeping?

"Yes, about fifty miles outside of Boston," Maria answers.

"And—" I stop abruptly on the sidewalk, eliciting a foul comment from a fellow pedestrian who has to swerve around me. I shake my head in disbelief at everything Maria's telling me. "I'm sorry, but this is a lot to take in— she left me in her estate?"

"You're the sole inheritor. But there are some stipula-tions." Maria sighs. "That's why it would be best if you came out here. Until we can get all this taken care of." A pause. "I'm not just Sybil's attorney—I was her friend. This was important to her, Rowan. You're important to her."

My chest tightens. If I was so important to Sybil, how could she lead a double life and keep it from me? Tears prick the corners of my eyes, but I take a deep breath and pull myself together. "I'll see you soon."

Twenty-four hours later, I pull my rental car into the tiny town of Raven's Roost. It's quaint, like something out of a fairy tale. Old Victorian houses. Picket fences. Flower boxes in windowsills. I roll down the window and let the warm May breeze into the car. Wood smoke and honeysuckle scent the air. I'm a *long* way from Los Angeles.

Following directions on the GPS, I continue through town and keep heading north. First, I travel through fields and orchards, then a thick forest rises up on each side of the road. I haven't been around this much nature since I was a girl. The heavy vice around my heart loosens. A little.

I turn left down a gravel driveway through the woods, and the trees close in around me. My window is still down, and now I smell earth and pine. I'm going to have to snap some pictures while I'm here. My fingers itch for my camera bag. Usually, I shoot city scenes and celebrity events, but wherever I go, I have to capture it on film. I live my life through my lens.

And then, abruptly, the house looms before me, around a bend in the driveway. It's enormous, made of dark gray stone like something out of a Jane Austen novel. One corner of the house is shaped like a tower, with a pointed pinnacle at the top, and a weathervane of a raven in flight. A wide set of steps lead up to the front door, and a covered veranda wraps around the side. Lush flowerbeds of rose, foxglove, and geranium lie out front, and the glass dome of an atrium rises behind the house.

Holy shit. Am I really inheriting this?

Maria said there were stipulations… and complications. Were the stipulations what complicated things, or is there something else? I guess I'm about to find out. Taking a deep breath, I park the car next to a black SUV and get out.

"Rowan!" Maria calls from the front steps. "I'm glad you found the place."

I stride up and extend my hand. "It's nice to meet you, Maria. Thank you for taking care of Sybil's estate."

Maria takes my hand and shakes it firmly. Her skin is warm, almost electric. She looks maybe a few years younger than Sybil, in her fifties, perhaps. Her eyes are friendly, the color of coffee, like her hair. As first impressions go, I decide I like her.

"I wish we weren't meeting like this," she says, a bitter smile on her face. "Sybil always talked about you. She cared for you like a daughter."

I nod, my lips flashing a forced smile. My mother died when I was three, and my father never found anyone else. He was too heartbroken to move on. Too heartbroken to do much of anything after that, including care for me and my brother. Sybil swooped in to help out. We spent every summer with her after that, until we were grown.

Staring up at the house, it feels like a knife in the gut. How could she have kept this from me? I feel betrayed all over again, like I had a year ago after walking in on my husband of ten years cavorting with his business partner.

Maria leads us to the covered veranda on the left and takes a seat in a white chair. She gestures to the seat next to her. "I have an office in town, but meeting at the house seemed more… well, I wanted you to see the place."

"Before we get into anything else," I say, my chair creaking beneath me as I sit down, "I need to know—what happened to her? When I got the call that Sybil had… they didn't give any details." I shake my head, tears fogging my throat. "She was so young."

"The coroner's office is working on that now," Maria says. "We should know something soon."

From where we're sitting, we have a view of a large walled garden and the forest beyond. I stare out into the expanse of green. "I'll need to start planning the funeral," I say. "Did she leave any details about that in her will? I'll need help with local vendors since I'm not familiar with this area." Details. If I focus on the details, my grief won't overwhelm me.

"She did leave instructions. I'll go over all that with you," Maria says with a nod. "We also need to go over the particulars of what she left you. The house and property— Raven Manor, it's called—for starters. And significant financial assets."

I shake my head. "It's so much to process. I—I never even knew she had a house here. A *life* here." Tears prick at the corners of my eyes, and I pull one knee up into the chair, hugging my arms around it.

"I know," Maria says softly. "And I'm sorry."

"You also mentioned complications?"

Something passes through Maria's eyes, and I can tell the other shoe is about to drop. "There's no way to say this except to just come out with it." She takes a deep breath, lets it back out. "Sybil—your aunt—well... she was a witch."

CHAPTER TWO

Rowan

"A witch?" I echo. I can feel my eyebrows arch so high they're practically touching my hairline.

"Yes," Maria says, nodding.

It's as if someone has taken my life and spun it like the roulette wheel at a casino. My brain is the little white ball, bouncing from one section to the next.

Everything in my life is one big lie.

But yet… flashbacks of my childhood fill my mind like the snaps of my camera lens. Sybil taking me outside to look at the full moon. A big black book she'd kept on her mahogany desk, with a crystal embedded in the cover. Groups of her female friends coming over for tea at her big house up in the hills in Sonoma, swapping flowers and herbs. Walking through the sun-drenched fields while Sybil talked to animals. I had laughed as a girl, thinking it was all for show. I'd loved Sybil for her eccentricity. She'd always been the fun grown-up in the family, when everyone else was so boring.

She may not have come out and said she was a witch, but she hadn't hidden it, either. Why hadn't I ever realized it before?

Maria reaches out and places a hand on mine. "You look like you're in shock."

"I'm… I'm okay," I say, though my voice trembles a bit. "I guess I knew all along, when I was a girl. But why did she have two homes? This one and her house in California?"

"Well, your aunt was very high-up in the witch community," Maria says. "We have covens, and there's also one overarching society. A group of witches that help others when the need arises. Sybil had two houses, one on the east coast, and one on the west, so she could attend to her duties."

"A society of witches?" I cock my head to the side as my thoughts spin again. One witch is mystifying enough, but a whole *society* of witches?

Maria nods. "The Raven Society."

"Raven Manor. And Raven's Roost. I assume that's no coincidence?" I could almost laugh. I want to laugh, want to pretend this is a practical joke.

"Correct. The Society started here in Massachusetts." Maria waves a hand around. "This house, in fact, is the headquarters of the Raven Society."

This keeps getting crazier by the moment. I can feel

my brain stretching to keep up with the impossibility of it all. "Sybil's house? Headquarters? So does that mean—"

"Yes, Rowan. Sybil was the leader of the Raven Society. High Priestess, as we call it."

It's the cherry on top of this wild conversation. My aunt was not only a witch, but there's a whole society of witches, and she was head of it all. Also, I don't miss Maria's choice of pronouns. "We?"

Another nod. "Yes. I'm a member as well."

"Attorney by day, sorceress by night." A bubble of slightly hysterical laughter escapes my lips.

"A sorceress is different, but close enough." Maria smiles.

My knuckles are white from gripping the arms of the chair too tightly. I shake my head. "This is all completely foreign to me."

"I get that. I'm sorry to have to go through all this when you're grieving your aunt." She frowns. "And I'm afraid that's not all."

My heart goes still, and I suck in a breath. There's *more?*

Maria hesitates before continuing. "You see, the stipulations I mentioned revolve around the house and the Raven Society."

"Oh. Sybil wants it to be used by the Society." I nod and my chest loosens a bit. If these witches want to use the house, that's fine by me. I just want to get out of this place as quickly as possible. This is all *far* too much for me. "Of course. This was important to her, and I totally respect that. I can make sure it's never sold and doesn't fall into disrepair."

"It's more than that," Maria says. "Since Sybil didn't have any daughters of her own, she wants her bloodline to be represented in the Society."

Maria pins me in a piercing gaze.

"But—you can't mean me?" I squeak. My relief from moments before dissipates. "Surely that person would have to be a witch?"

Maria's intense eyes remain locked on mine.

"I'm *not* a witch. Clearly." I laugh, because I'm not sure what else to do. I feel like I've entered the Twilight Zone. Maybe I'm so grief stricken I'm having delusions?

"You are a Stonecroft woman. You possess magic, no doubt about it."

"I think I would know," I say, crossing my arms over my chest. There's an uncomfortable heat building in my stomach, and my head starts to throb. Abruptly, I reach my limit. The last of my sanity is going over a cliff any moment now. "Listen, it's been a really terrible couple of days. Can we pick this conversation up again in the morning?"

"Of course," Maria says with a comforting smile. "I assume you're planning to stay here at the house?"

I hadn't actually given it any thought. I'd simply packed a suitcase and hopped on the next cross-country flight I could find. Perks of being self-employed and single.

"Um, sure," I say. The place is soothing. I can feel

Sybil's presence, even here on the outside of the house. Maybe if I spend some time here, I can come to terms with the fact that my aunt wasn't who I thought she was at all. I can process my grief, and then I can get out of here and try to move on with my life. Without broomsticks and magic and other things far beyond my comprehension.

"Great, well, here's a key."

Maria reaches into her purse and pulls out a huge, ornate iron key, which she hands over. It's cold against my skin and I shiver.

"Also, there's another tenant at the moment," Maria continues. "The Society offers a place for witches to stay when they're down on their luck. She's staying in the moon room."

I don't know what a moon room is, and I'm too tired and overwhelmed to ask at this point. "Great, okay. I'll see you tomorrow then."

Maria nods and heads out to her SUV, throwing me a final wave before driving off. A breeze rustles through the forest, stirring the scent of something flowering. I can hear the squeak of the weathervane overhead as it spins, and I wrap my arms around myself. How had everything in my life gotten so crazy so fast?

With a sigh, I turn, looking up at the enormous front door. It's painted burgundy, a pop against the gray of the rest of the house. Inserting the key into the lock, which has to be wrestled into submission, I open it and stare into the yawning space beyond.

The house sparkles with a strange golden light, which a

moment later I realize is just a trick of the sun and dust motes. A big stained-glass window, which I hadn't noticed from the outside, is letting in a good bit of illumination. There's a skylight in the middle of the roof as well, three stories up. I don't like dark old houses, so that makes me feel better.

At the far end of the two-story foyer, which is really more of a wide hall, a wooden staircase curves up and around, leading to the second floor. The mahogany banister gleams. I can see that it continues up to the third floor, perhaps an attic? From the outside, it had seemed the third floor was much smaller. I walk further in, seeing a huge dining room with a fireplace to the left, and a sitting room on the right. Further still, and I see a parlor with a giant harp, and beyond that, a kitchen that looks like something right out of Tuscany: brightly-colored tile, huge stone oven and all.

There are other rooms downstairs, but I leave those for later exploration and head up the staircase to the second floor. Paintings cover the polished wood walls, most of them depicting enigmatic women, or nature, or the moon. And several of ravens, naturally. As if tugged by a magnetic force, I make my way around the rectangular-shaped hall, which has a handrail on the interior and is open to the first floor. I pass four bedrooms before stopping at the fifth. The door is open, and I step inside.

It's Sybil's room, of that I have no doubt. The four-poster bed is set with a turquoise quilt, her favorite color, and on top of the dresser sits a vase filled with sunflowers, also a favorite. But it's more than that. I can *feel* her here. I cross the room to a saffron satin chair and sit down in it. My eyes rove over the space, every book and nick-knack. There's a chenille throw on the arm of the chair which I pull into my lap.

And then my exhaustion takes me.

———

Moonlight is streaming in through the window when I awaken. I instantly realize I'm not alone. My whole body goes on alert, and my eyes land on a tall shadow in the doorway to Sybil's room.

"I'm so sorry!"

A woman steps into the light. She looks a bit younger than my thirty-five years and has long, flaming red hair and strange purple eyes that burn in the dim light. Smoke curls up from something in her hands. "I didn't mean to wake you. But I have tea, if you want." She smiles and takes a few tentative steps forward, proffering the steaming mug.

I reach out and take it. "Thanks so much. I'm Rowan."

"I'm Lavender," she says. "Ven for short. Maria told you I'm staying here?"

"Yeah, she did." I shake my head. "Sorry I didn't come introduce myself before I passed out. I was exhausted from my flight and then a bit…well, Maria told me some things I wasn't aware of. Just a lot to take in."

"Oh, about all of us being witches?"

I tense for a moment, then nod and take a sip of my tea. Mint and chamomile. "Um, yep. That would be it."

Ven takes a seat at the end of Sybil's bed. "Yeah. I bet that's some crazy shit to hear right after you step off a plane." She giggles.

Her laughter is infectious, and I find myself joining in. "You can say that again." I take another sip of my tea.

"Sybil told me so much about you." Ven smiles. "I feel like we're already friends."

I nod, not sure what to say since I can't return the sentiment, having never heard of her before. Grief stabs my gut once again. Luckily, she continues without much of a pause.

"I'll always owe Sybil a debt of gratitude. I was in a bad coven before, and a bad relationship. She took me in, offered me protection." Her eyes hold a far-off look for a moment, as if lost in her memories. "I know you must be going through a lot right now, and I'll help you any way I can. Any kin of Sybil is good in my book."

"Thanks, Ven," I say with a smile.

A loud banging sound moves through the house, and it takes me a moment to realize it's someone knocking on the front door. "What time is it?" I ask, brow crinkled.

"After eleven." Ven wears a frown and a furrow same as mine.

We get up and walk together downstairs. As I approach the door, I can see, through the narrow decorative glass panels on each side, a looming shape. I pause in front of the door.

"Who is it?" I call.

"Sheriff's office," booms a male voice.

I look to Ven, and she nods. "I recognize him. That's the sheriff."

I open the door and look up into dark eyes at least eight inches above my head. And at five eight, I'm not exactly short. The sheriff is solid muscle, with a sweep of thick blonde hair. Probably handsome by most standards, if I were into the law enforcement type.

"Can I help you?" I ask.

"You must be Rowan Stonecroft," he says, his tone gruff.

I nod. As of last week, when the divorce papers were signed, I am a Stonecroft once again.

"I'm Sheriff Johnson. Sorry to bother you so late." He dips his hat. "I'm afraid I have rather urgent news, however. Your aunt's autopsy report came back."

Ven steps up beside me and shoots me a sidelong glance.

"We found poison in her system," he says.

"Poison?" Adrenaline shoots through my veins. "What exactly are you saying?"

The sheriff's gaze sweeps over Ven and back to me. "What I'm saying is that your aunt's death is now a murder investigation."

CHAPTER THREE

Rowan

As soon as the sun lightens the sky, I climb out of bed. I hadn't been asleep. How could anyone sleep after getting news that their aunt had been murdered?

The sheriff had said that suicide had to be ruled out as well, though Ven and I assured him that we didn't think that was a possibility. Sybil had never struggled with depression; she'd always been happy and care-free. He'd promised to keep us posted and disappeared into the night. Which had left me staring at the ceiling for hours, trying to calm the racing of my heart.

So, as soon as day breaks, I get dressed in yoga pants, a tank top, and running shoes. I don't know where I'm going to go, I just know I have to get out of this house, and I have to be alone. As soon as I step out onto the front steps a cool breeze blows, as if the forest is calling to me.

How long has it been since I walked in an actual forest? Somehow, my life had become this concrete prison in LA, never leaving the crush and bustle of the city.

I walk out into the yard and head into the trees, moving away from the road. Hopefully away from any neighbors, too. Not that I can see any in these dense woods. My feet move of their own volition and I begin to jog. Before long, I can feel my muscles warm up. It feels good to move. To be free.

My head space has been completely wack for the last year. First, finding out my husband was cheating. Nearly a year of dealing with that drama: attorneys, separating households, fighting over who got to keep what, as if he had any right after what he'd done. In the end, I'd let him buy me out of my portion of the house and everything in it. I didn't want to take any of our stuff with me anyway. Too many memories I no longer wanted.

And just when I thought the bad times were behind me, just when I thought I was free, this had happened. Sybil had died, murdered no less. What the hell had I done to create all this bad karma?

I'm running before I realize it. Full out, arms and legs pumping, heart galloping in my chest, lungs burning. The forest is a blur around me, nothing but a world of emerald and sage and peridot. I let it all burn out of me, every bit of rage and shock and sorrow. Sweat it out through my pores, pound it out with my footsteps.

When I finally stop, exhausted, I have no idea where I am. There are still no houses to be seen. I'm in the absolute middle of nowhere. And I'm thirsty as hell. But I don't regret it.

As if the forest is taking pity on me, I hear a trickle of water and follow the sound. My eyes widen as I come around a grove of trees and see a waterfall coming down a small cliff, probably a dozen feet high. The water spills over several boulders before forming into a pool at the base, and then continuing as a tiny stream meandering through the woods. The sun, which has now risen substantially higher, glints across it, and dragonflies flit over the surface. It's breathtakingly beautiful, but more importantly, it looks like exactly the thing to cool me off.

There's no one around, so I strip off my tank top and throw it into the grass at my feet. My sneakers follow it, and I tip-toe forward to dip my feet in the water.

That's when something steps out from behind the waterfall, parting the sheets of water like a curtain.

Not something, but someone. And not someone, but a man.

A man who is wearing not a lick of clothing.

He's tall and rippling with muscle like a Roman statue. The water streams off of him, plastering his black hair away from his face. He's got a jawline that could cut a diamond, and his eyes are the oddest shade of gold I've ever seen. He has to be wearing contacts.

I'm completely gawking when he flicks those golden eyes over to me. At which point I realize that I'm standing here in nothing but my bra and yoga pants, alone in the middle of the woods with a strange, naked man.

And yet I can't force myself to look away from him.

He stares at me with an unreadable expression, eyes roving over me. Drinking me in, like I'm drinking him in. He doesn't seem the least bit uncomfortable that he's nude, and the cold water hasn't shrunken *anything*. In fact, as he stares at me the substantial length of it begins to grow, and I feel the first flicker of fear.

We stand like that for several breaths, staring. Then he lets out a low growl and turns away from me abruptly. He strides off into the trees, and a moment later, he's gone.

WANT TO BE AN AUTHOR'S BEST FRIEND?

Blood, sweat, tears, wine, and a little piece of my soul went into writing this book. I'd love to know what you think! Leave a review on Goodreads and your book retailer of choice. Tell me your favorite character or your favorite scene. Reviews help authors a ton, both in ranking algorithms and making a living, so I much appreciate it! You can also email me a note or send fan art (I LOVE fan art!) to auroragreyauthor@gmail.com

And come chat with me on Facebook, Instagram, TikTok, or BookBub!

ABOUT THE AUTHOR

 Aurora Grey lives in Florida with her dog, too many cats, and a very mischievous horse. She writes stories about magic, swoonworthy dudes, and the strong, sexy women they fall for. When not enjoying books, she can be found traveling, a glass of champagne in hand.

Keep up with ALL the latest news! Sign up for Aurora's newsletter on her website:
www.AuroraGreyAuthor.com

She also likes to hang on:
Instagram: instagram.com/auroragreyauthor
TikTok: tiktok.com/@auroragreyauthor
Facebook: facebook.com/auroragreyauthor
Reader Group: https://www.facebook.com/groups/
457978148823608
BookBub: bookbub.com/authors/aurora-grey

Printed in Great Britain
by Amazon

42551483R00179